2018
3rd Place
PUBLISHED FICTION

The New Darkness won Third Place in the Published Fiction Category of the 2018 Arizona Authors Association Annual Literary Contest. The contest has been open to authors in all states for several years. The seven judges all rated the writing with top marks.

Praise For
THE BLUESUIT CHRONICLES

"The first installment of The Bluesuit Chronicles, (*The War Comes Home*) is a compelling start to what is sure to be an epic saga. A former Golden Gloves boxer and Army medic return home from Vietnam to a very different America than the one he left. The drug craze of the early seventies takes a heavy toll on the Boomer generation, and the social fabric begins to unravel, nail-biting action, romance, and intrigue, based on actual events." Rated Four Stars.
~ Red City Reviews

"From the moment I started reading *The War Comes Home*, I couldn't put it down. I was captivated by the balance of action and drama that John Hansen expertly weaves throughout this fast-paced historical fiction. I'm looking forward to reading the next one."
~ S. McDonald, Redmond, WA

John Hansen
2021

Praise For
THE BLUESUIT CHRONICLES

"An exciting, read, riveting action, romance and moving scenes. *The War Comes Home* took me back to the Bellevue I knew in 'the good old days.' Impossible to put down." ~ Cynthia Davis, Bellevue, WA

"*The War Comes Home* follows the activities of two city police officers, Hitchcock and Walker, as they prepare and then head out for the nightly patrol of their Neighborhood streets. Hitchcock feels a strange foreboding that there will be danger that evening, and someone will die. The two police officers spend the evening patrolling areas looking for drug dealers, prostitutes, and other criminals.

This manuscript is extremely well-written. The author has infused the prose with an interesting mix of dialogue, inner thoughts. The characters are nicely developed, the dialogue is genuine and flows organically. The reader is immediately drawn into the story and wants to learn more, not only about the officers, but what awaits them as they begin their nightly patrol." ~ Review by an editor at Bookbaby

"I wish there were more chapters, John. I could not put *The War Comes Home* down. Not only was it very well written but I began to imagine not only what I would do but how that moment in police work would cope with the different times. Can't wait until the next one. ~ Officer Nathan Vance, Bonney Lake Police Department, Bonney Lake, WA

"Book Two of The Bluesuit Chronicles series, *The New Darkness*, continues the story of Vietnam veteran Roger Hitchcock, now a police officer in Bellevue, Washington. The spreading new drug culture is taking a heavy toll on Hitchcock's generation. Some die, some are permanently impaired, everyone is impacted by this wave of evil that even turns traditional values inside out. Like other officers, the times test Hitchcock: will he resign in disgust, become hardened and bitter, corrupt, or will his background in competition boxing and military combat experience enable him to rise to meet the challenge? Romance, intrigue and action are the fabric of *The New Darkness*."

Praise For
THE BLUESUIT CHRONICLES

"*Valley of Long Shadows* is the third book in The Bluesuit Chronicles... Returning Vietnam veterans who become police officers find themselves holding the line against societal anarchy. Even traditional roles between cops and robbers in police work have become more deadly...The backdrop is one of government betrayal, societal breakdown, and an angry disillusioned public. The '70s is the decade that brought America where it is now.
Four Stars Rating ~ Red City Reviews

"Received Book 4, *Day Shift* on a Wednesday. Already done reading it. Couldn't help myself. Was only going to read a couple chapters and save the rest for my upcoming camping trip. LOL. 3 hours later book finished. Love it. 2 Thumbs up !!! ~ Alanda Bailey, Kalispell, MT

"By the time I finished reading the series up through Book Four (*Day Shift*), I concluded most men would like to be Hitchcock, at least in some way. What sets him apart is the dichotomy of his makeup: he grew up with a Boy Scout sense of honor and right and wrong, yet he isn't hardened or jaded by the evil and cruelty he saw when he went to war, though he killed in combat. As a policeman he *chooses* good and right: to do otherwise is unthinkable. He is a skilled fighter, yet so modest that he doesn't know he is a role model for others around him, and women feel safe with him. I know Hitchcock's type—two of my relatives were cops who influenced my life:"
~ Tracy Smith, Newcastle, WA

"Book Five (*Unfinished Business*) moves to show how difficult it is for Officer Hitchcock to do right. Bad people are out to get him for his good work. He is a threat to their nefarious activities. There is even a very bad high-ranking policeman who puts Hitchcock and his family in extreme peril. Organized foreign crime is moving into his city, he works hard to uncover the clues to solve this evil in his city. I'm still waiting to find out what restaurant owner Juju is up to and who she works for. Great series and story. Another fine book by John Hansen. Yo! ~ T.A. Smith

Praise For
THE BLUESUIT CHRONICLES

"I received the 5th book in The Bluesuit Chronicles and started reading and per usual, didn't stop until I finished the book. I am a huge fan of John's stories. I grew up in the general area that the stories are set in. Also, in the same time frame. John's books are always fast paced and entertaining reads. I would recommend them to any and all."
~ A. Bailey-Kalispell, MT

"John Hansen has written another great read. *Unfinished Business* is filled with conspiracy, corruption and crime, much of which is targeted at Hitchcock. From the beginning of the book I was hooked. The author has a gift with words that drew me into the story effortlessly. I could not put the book down. I have read all in the series and I look forward to reading more of John Hansen's books." ~ S. McDonald

"I urge you to complete your 'to do' list prior to reading *Unfinished Business*, as once started, I could not put it down. It was always, 'one more page' and soon I was not getting anything else done, but it was well worth it. The author has an amazing way of drawing the reader into each scene, adding to the excitement, sweet romance, raw emotion and revealing of each fascinating character as the plots unfold. I highly recommend this book to anyone who wants a truly good read. Looking forward to the next book from this highly talented author." ~ Cynthia R.

"I've read all of John's books and rated them all 5 stars, because those stars are earned. I worked the street with John as a police officer for years and what he speaks of in his books is real. John is an excellent author; articulate and clear, always bringing the reader directly into the story. I like John's work to the point that I've asked him to send me any new books he writes; I'll be either the first or almost the first to read all of them. I lived this with John. He's an author not to be missed. You can't go wrong reading his books. I strongly encourage more in the series." ~ Bill Cooper, Chief of Police (ret)

Praise For
THE BLUESUIT CHRONICLES

"A viewpoint from the inside: I worked with and partnered with John both in uniform and in detectives, and like him I came to the Department after military service. This is the fifth (as of this date) of five books in this series. I have read and re-read all five books, and for the first time, recently, over a two-day period, read the entire series in order. All five books were inspired by John's experiences, during many of which I was present. John is an extremely gifted author and I was transported back to those times and experienced a full gamut of emotions, mostly good, sometimes less so. His use of humor, love, anger, fear, camaraderie, loyalty, respect, disapproval, devotion, and other emotions, rang true throughout the books." ~ Robert Littlejohn

"The whole series of The Bluesuit Chronicles brought back a flood of memories. I started in police work in 1976. This series starts a couple of years earlier. The descriptions of the equipment, the way you had to solve crimes without the assistance of modern items. John made me feel that I was there when it was happening. This whole series is what police work is about. Working with citizens, caring about them, and catching the bad guys. Officers in that time period cared about what they did. It wasn't all about a paycheck... We were the originators of community policing. We knew our beat and the people in it. I am not saying we were perfect; however, we were very committed to our community. That being said, I can't wait for the next book. Please read the whole series. Once you start you won't stop."
~ Garry C. Dixon, Ret. LEO-Virginia

"Retired Detective John Hansen is a master writer. He brings to life policing in the Northwestern U.S. during the '70s; a transitional period. One has to wonder of how much of his writings are founded in personal experience vs. creative thinking. Either way, his stories are thoroughly enjoyable and well-worth purchasing his original books in this series, his current release, as well as the books yet to come."
~ Debbie M.-Scottsdale, AZ

Also by John Hansen:

The Award -Winning Series: The Bluesuit Chronicles:

The War Comes Home
The New Darkness
Valley of Long Shadows
Day Shift
Unfinished Business
The Mystery of the Unseen Hand

Published & Award -Winning Essays and Short Stories:

"Losing Kristene"
"Riding the Superstitions"
"The Case of the Old Colt"
"Charlie's Story"
"The Mystery of Three"
"The Prospector"

Non-Fiction Book:
Song of the Waterwheel

The New Darkness

Book 2 of The Bluesuit Chronicles

JOHN HANSEN

The New Darkness
by John Hansen

This book is a work of fiction. Names, characters, locations and events are either a product of the author's imagination, fictitious or used fictitiously. Any resemblance to any event, locale or person, living or dead, is purely coincidental.

Third Edition
Revised and Reprinted - Copyright © 2020 John Hansen
Original Copyright © 2017 John Hansen

Cover Designer: Jessica Bell - Jessica Bell Design
Interior Design and Formatting: Deborah J Ledford - IOF Productions Ltd

Issued in Print and Electronic Formats
Trade Paperback ISBN: 978-1735803012

Manufactured in the United States of America

The New Darkness

JOHN HANSEN

To Patricia, my heart, my passion, my crown,
all my love, always.

This series is dedicated to the men and women who answered the call to serve and protect, whether in a military or law enforcement capacity, so others can sleep at night.

~ John Hansen

"The world will not be destroyed by those who do evil, but by those who watch them without doing anything."

~ Albert Einstein

PROLOGUE

OF THE PILLARS of society in Everett, Washington, the Masconi family had no peers. Their mansion in Boulevard Bluffs, the city's most upscale neighborhood, featured a commanding view of Possession Sound. Luca Masconi, the head of the family, was a senior partner in one of the Northwest's most prestigious law firms.

Mr. Masconi specialized in maritime law, which required him to be knowledgeable on legal matters which occurred on U.S. and international waters. His wife, Sophia, in addition to running a busy household of five children, a nanny and two live-in maids, was also active in the church and a variety of charities.

All five children attended prestigious Catholic schools from kindergarten to high school and college. The eldest of the Masconi children, and the pride of the clan was Claudia. The brightest of her siblings, Claudia's grades were always straight A or A minus, no matter the subject.

1

Through her mother's influence, Claudia was steeped in traditional family values – a second nanny to her siblings, her mama's right hand in helping with bathing, changing diapers, feeding, potty-training, and reading bedtime stories. She did these duties in addition to helping her mother and the maid with laundry, house-cleaning, and cooking family-size meals. Such responsibilities Claudia met cheerfully, for giving and caring was her nature.

Unlike most girls her age, Claudia wasn't a fan of the Beatles. She preferred the music of black musicians like Ray Charles, Jimi Hendrix and Aretha Franklin. She admired Che Guevarra, the Cuban revolutionary, but this she hid from her parents, knowing they regarded Guevarra as a communist and a murderer.

More than her reputation for wholesomeness, good character and integrity, which preceded her in the community, was Claudia's beauty. Her paternal and maternal lineage was of northern Italy, her hair was a light shade of auburn; lustrous, wavy and thick. Her blue almond-shaped eyes were set in olive skin and high cheekbones like glowing sapphires. Figure-wise she was tall, long-legged and statuesque, and many were the men who asked her on dates, but she seldom accepted, for as she told her friends, she was saving herself for her future husband.

Through academic excellence and participation in team sports, Claudia won a scholarship to Seattle

University, a Catholic college run by Jesuit priests located east of Seattle's downtown core, between the International District and the Central District. She entered Seattle U intent on fulfilling her compassion for minorities and the less fortunate by becoming a civil rights lawyer in a big city law firm on the East Coast.

One Friday night of the beginning of Claudia's sophomore year, she and two other female classmates from her sociology class decided to go bar hopping to see the less fortunate classes for themselves. It was a daring adventure for three well-bred young ladies who came from stable, devout, educated, upper-crust stock.

They ate and drank cocktails in Chinatown first, taking in the rough atmosphere, flirting with men of very different cultures than theirs. As the evening wore on, and alcohol lowered their inhibitions, they decided to visit bars in the Central District.

They were nervous when they entered a dark, ramshackle bar off the beaten path from Rainier Avenue, crowded with dark-skinned, rowdy, forward, working class young men. The two classmates were nice looking girls, but they didn't compare with Claudia's beauty. Within seconds, men hovered around Claudia, ignoring her two friends. Their attention to her made her nervous, for she and her friends were the only white people there. Her only exposure to minorities were to her family's Filipino maids, and the gardener, which she now realized were transactional relationships.

As the evening wore on and alcohol lowered their inhi-bitions, the trio naively giggled and flirted with the working-class men. Claudia, having been drinking all night, grew increasingly more fascinated, for men like these were outside her experience. The only eligible men she had been exposed to were white, well-dressed, well-schooled and mild-mannered.

Then, to Claudia's surprise, she noticed two young white women who arrived and sat at another table. The dark-skinned, rowdy men who surrounded them seemed to know them. Claudia was fascinated. One girl was demure and slim, the other a crude, chunky blonde with a bold aspect in her eyes. She stared at Claudia.

It amazed Claudia that these white women seemed so comfortable with where they were. She told her friends she had to go to the restroom. Tipsy on her feet, she threaded her way to the table where the two white women sat, at the far end of the bar, through the dense crowd of rough men, flirting with them as she leaned upon one, then another to keep from falling.

After fifteen minutes had passed and Claudia had not returned, one of her friends threaded her way through the crowd of men to the ladies' room, now nervous amid jeering, groping men. The crude remarks of these men made her more nervous with every step, for no one had ever spoken to her as these men did.

Claudia's friends didn't find her in the ladies' room. Bewildered, they asked everyone where Claudia had

4

gone. But the only answer anyone gave them was, "She left, went out the back."

"Who did she leave with?" one of her classmates asked the rough men in working clothes who were hanging out, with beers in their hands, by the back door. They exchanged glances with each other, smirked and shrugged their shoulders, indicating they had knowledge to the disadvantage of Claudia and her friends.

Claudia's friends began to panic as they looked for her in the cars and trucks in the parking lot to no avail. They returned to the bar and waited until the owner told the customer he would be closing soon.

Rather than leave, Claudia's friends called the police. Two uniformed officers and a sergeant arrived in minutes. Upon speaking with Claudia's friends, silence fell over the bar as the sergeant shut the doors. No one was allowed to leave until every man inside had been identified and questioned, including the bartender.

The officers searched the restrooms, back office, and the storage room. The sergeant directed one of the officers to check inside every car in the gravel parking lot. When the officer returned and shook his head, the sergeant hooked his thumbs in his gunbelt as he turned to Claudia's friends. "What brought three college girls from out of town down here?" He asked in a demanding tone. "Were you slumming—amusing yourselves with working people? Were you comfortable being the only females here?"

"Oh, no, we aren't the only women here," one of the friends replied. "There were two other women–" The friend stopped as she looked around. "They're gone!"

"Who's gone?" the sergeant asked.

"There were two other white women sitting at that table right there," the other friend said, "I didn't see them leave, either."

The sergeant questioned the bartender, who denied seeing other women in the bar. The customers, all men, also said they didn't see or didn't remember seeing two other white women.

Detectives took up the case days later. They re-interviewed the bar patrons who were there that night, and went through credit card receipts for names of customers who had been at the bar before Claudia's friends called the police, but after two weeks of following up on customers who had been at the bar that night and extensive questioning of the bartender, the bar owners, Claudia's two friends, they never solved Claudia's disappearance. In desperation her family called the news media.

The case made local headlines in print and television. Investigative reporters tried their best to find her, but to no avail. Claudia had vanished without a trace.

CHAPTER ONE
Moonlight Madness

Bellevue, Washington
September 16, 1970
Wednesday - 8:05 P.M.

THE HUNGARIAN GORILLA, the man officers made such remarks about as "One of these nights we'll find the whole family dead," "Inhuman strength," "Took three of us to take him down," was at it again. And Hitchcock was on his way to meet him for the first time.

Under moonlight bright enough to read a newspaper, he sped Code Two in and out of ghostly shadows along the winding curves of Richards Road to the house where Sherman waited outside.

Fearing a homicide in progress, Hitchcock sped as fast as he dared, keeping both hands on the wheel. His rotating roof-mounted emergency light cast an eerie red glow on the tunnel of trees and dense vegetation on both sides of the road.

His radio crackled. He heard urgency in Sherman's voice.

"Again–your ETA, Three Zero Six?"

Hitchcock dared to take one hand off the steering wheel to key his mic. "One minute."

His very first call came to mind as he entered the neighborhood. It was on this same street, three houses down, exactly a year ago, riding shotgun with Sergeant Lane Baxter, under another full moon. A terrified mother and two children in blood-stained clothes, huddled at the edge of the driveway.

The husband in the basement, prancing and chanting in a strange language, wearing a full-length, hooded, red satin robe, a bloody knife in his hand, bowing before a horned image on the fireplace mantle. The family dog dead at his feet, its throat cut. The grisly battle to arrest him stunned Hitchcock, an experienced boxer and combat veteran.

THE BRAKE LIGHTS of Sherman's black-and-white cruiser, a 1970 Plymouth Fury, flashed once to signal his location.

Hitchcock pulled up behind him and got out. Sherman, as tall as Hitchcock but on a lighter frame, had the wiry strength and toughness of a gymnast. He nodded toward the Northwest-style split-level home across the street, where lights were on inside and bedsheets covered the large living room windows.

They listened for noises inside the house but heard nothing. A bad sign. Hitchcock gave an inquiring nod to Sherman.

"They're Hungarian immigrants," Sherman explained in a low voice. "The old man is a boozer, big, very strong, brutal, loves to fight. The first full moon stirs him up every time. Walker and I arrested him last month for beating up his wife and teenage son. We fought him out of the house, into the patrol car and every step of the way to the booking room."

"So I've heard," Hitchcock said. "Hear anything else while I was on my way?"

"Nothing after the wife's scream, followed by a crash."

"Let's hope the reason for the quiet isn't because she's dead."

"I hope you ate your Wheaties this morning, Roger, 'cause you're gonna need 'em," Sherman said.

The former boxer flashed a confident grin. Sherman shook his head and smiled.

Hitchcock noted the paint peeling from the front door, the bedsheets for living room curtains, and a grimy welcome mat; indications of financial distress. They positioned themselves on either side of the door and leaned close to listen. A blaring television overrode the sounds of a man and a woman arguing. The woman was sobbing.

The doorbell didn't work. Sherman knocked. No answer. Sherman knocked louder this time. "Police officers! Open the door!" No response. The door was unlocked.

"Police officers! We're coming in!" Sherman yelled.

They heard the indistinct crying of a woman as they stepped inside. No one was visible. They waited at the bottom of the stairs.

A moment later a disheveled, middle aged woman, dressed in a tattered cotton dress, her salt-and-pepper hair in a tangle, defeat etched deep into the lines of her face, appeared at the top of the stairs. She covered her mouth with her hand, her left eye was black and almost swollen shut. Hitchcock climbed the stairs and gently checked her face, noting defense wounds on her forearms.

"What happened, Katalin?" Sherman asked. "Who did this to you? Was it–?"

"Yaus. Lajos, who ulse?" she sobbed in her thick Eastern European accent.

"Where is he? Where are the children?"

"Children hiding downstairs, afraid! Lajos in da' den, down hall, dat way," she said, indicating the location with a nod.

Hitchcock checked her pupils with his flashlight. "Your pupils are uneven. That means you have a head injury, ma'am. Are your kids hurt?"

Katalin shook her head.

"Let's get you and your kids out of the house and to the hospital. I hear the guys from the funeral home are outside now," Sherman said.

Hitchcock guarded the hallway in case Lajos attacked while Sherman escorted Katalin and her children filed out of the house.

Katalin blinked her one good eye at Sherman and Hitchcock as she held her hand over her bleeding mouth. "Lajos, he wait for you, he know I call you, he want fight you, he say he will beat *you* this time," she muttered.

Sherman guided Katalin and her two children to the driveway. Hitchcock could hear the television in the den where Lajos was. He heard the hearse from Flintoff's Mortuary in the driveway, then two doors slam.

Sherman returned. "The guys from Flintoff's are treating the mom before they take her and the kids to the hospital," he said.

"Did she at least flinch when she saw it's a hearse that's taking her to the ER, not an ambulance?"

"Nah. They've ridden to the ER with the boys from Flintoff's before. They're used to it."

"It's tank time for Lajos," Hitchcock said, finality in his voice. "You've been through this with him before, so what's the plan?"

"We make a calm approach on either side from behind, if we can. He's strong as a bull, even stronger than he looks. We'll pin his arms to his sides the second he starts to resist, which he will do, then take him to the floor and cuff him."

"That's it?" Hitchcock asked, somewhat incredulous.

Sherman smirked. "That'll be just the *beginning*."

"Ready when you are," Hitchcock said.

"One more thing: Lajos is crafty. He played possum with Walker and me last month so we'd try to sweet-talk him into going with us peaceably. As soon as he saw our guard was down, he attacked. If not for Walker, I'd have ended up in the hospital."

"Anything else?"

"The second he balks at our instructions, and he will, talk is over. We take him down quick."

"Sounds like a plan, Stan, let's go,"

Hitchcock pointed at two large breaks in the sheetrock walls of the hallway as he followed Sherman to the den. "These from last time?" he asked.

"Yep, the guy's cheap," Sherman nodded.

"Bet he leaves the damage to remind his wife and kids not to cross him."

Sherman opened the closed door of the den. Hitchcock followed him in. Lajos sat in a busted-down brown vinyl recliner, feet up, his back to the door, watching a commercial for Chesterfield cigarettes on the black-and-white television. Csizmadia's head turned slightly at the sound of footsteps behind him.

One glance explained the gorilla nickname. His

arms were long, with thick, ropy muscles, covered with dark hair, ending with ham-like hands. His head was supported by a short, furry stump of a neck, which sloped into broad shoulders laden with muscle. His short forehead angled back from heavy brows to his hairline. Thick wads of muscle bulged and tufts of hair poked through holes in his filthy white T-shirt. He stank of beer, cigarettes and stale sweat. His khaki pants were grimy, his hairy potbelly protruded past his belt.

He tilted his head back, opened his square, jutting jaw and let out a loud belch, releasing an almost visible cloud of foul air as he held a stubby brown bottle of Olympia beer in his hand. He kept his eyes on the television, smirking, ignoring Hitchcock and Sherman. Empty brown beer bottles and caps littered the floor on both sides of his chair. A half-empty pack of Pall Mall cigarettes, a Zippo lighter and an overflowing ashtray almost covered the side table next to him.

A few seconds of uneasy silence passed. Hitchcock watched Czismadia pick up a fresh bottle of beer, the kind that didn't have a twist-off cap, and use his thumb to flick the cap off with almost no effort. *He's psyching us up to fight him,* Hitchcock thought as he and Sherman positioned themselves on either side of and behind Lajos. The bloody scuff marks on Lajos's knuckles didn't escape Hitchcock's notice.

"Lajos, your wife has head injuries, Sherman said. "Says you hit her. We want to hear your side of it."

"Yeh, she's always bitchin' 'bout somethin'. You know how it is wi' wimmen," he snickered. "No udder way to shut 'em up," he said with a shrug of his shoulders and a grin. He took another swig of beer, then smiled as he belched again.

Lajos glanced up at Hitchcock, who stood over him, glaring. "Wot th' hell do you thenk you are doing, staring at me like dat, eh?"

Hitchcock stared down at Czismadia like a judge about to render a guilty verdict. Raised by his father in the knightly code championing the weak, women in particular, his hair-trigger wrath for men who beat women was the Achilles Heel in his professionalism.

Itching for a fight, he jeered at Czismadia. "Just wondering what kind of man hits his wife. No real *man* does that. Only lowdown *cowards* like *you* beat women!" Hitchcock answered in a taunting tone.

Lajos turned and looked Hitchcock up and down. He turned his head as he snorted dismissively. "So wat, eh?"

Sherman had been on DV calls with Hitchcock before. He rolled his eyes and shook his head when Hitchcock leaned over and whispered in a mocking tone, "You like to beat women? And little children too, I bet! Only low-down *cowards* do that!" Hitchcock shouting in Czismadia's ear.

An evil grin spread across gorilla's face. "Yah? Let me remind you—this is *my* house you are in, officer! You go out my house or I weel throw you both out!" He set his beer on the side table and his feet on the floor.

Sherman raised his hands to indicate no threat. "Hold on, Lajos. We're leaving, all right, but you'll have to go with us. You're under arrest for assault. You have the right to remain silent. Anything you say will–"

Sherman never finished the Miranda warnings. The second he touched Lajos's left arm, the fight was on.

"*Nem! Ez alkalommal fogom verni titeket!*" Csizmadia shouted, Hungarian for: 'No! This time I will beat you both!' Growling like a bear, he leaped out of his recliner, attacking both Sherman and Hitchcock by throwing wild punches.

They rushed him on either side, crashing over the wood coffee table and the television console. After a full minute of wrestling they managed to get Lajos face-down on the floor, and pinned his arms to his sides.

Lajos continued fighting with his feet, kicking and twisting his trunk to break free. He was even stronger than he appeared. He bellowed and grunted, sounding like an enraged bull. "*Ahhh! Uhhh! Uhhh!*" Each blast from his lungs stank worse than his body odor and seemed to increase his strength.

Holding Csizmadia's left arm against his body, Hitchcock on the right, Sherman motioned to Hitchcock to help get Csizmadia's arms behind his back. Csizmadia craned his neck and snapped his teeth like a rabid dog in an effort to bite Hitchcock's hand.

Hitchcock pulled his hand out of the way, escaping being bitten by less than an inch. He placed his right knee between Csizmadia's shoulder blades, pressing every ounce of his hundred ninety-five pounds into his upper back while Sherman pulled his wrists together and snapped the cuffs on.

His face squished into the carpet, gasping for breath under Hitchcock's weight, Csizmadia relaxed. "Okay, boys, yeh, I give up, I give up. I fight no more. You boys win again," he said between gasps. Neither Hitchcock nor Sherman could see him smiling.

Csizmadia's face was a picture of glee when they stood him up. "Lajos," Sherman said, "the law says we have to take you to jail. Will you go with us without any more trouble?"

The veins of his bull neck bulged like blue hoses under his skin, black greasy hair covered his eyes, his foul breath polluted the air from heavy panting. He gave an evil smile at Sherman and nodded as he waited to catch his breath. Sherman caught Hitchcock's attention and shook his head to convey his thought, *no way is this guy done.*

Hitchcock nodded his understanding. He placed his right hand on Csizmadia's right arm and his left hand at the base of the neck in order to know in advance if Lajos would spring into another attack.

The three moved forward. The Hungarian's shoulders tensed when they reached the door. Bending from the waist, he spun halfway around and charged Hitchcock, knocking him against the wall. Hitchcock recovered and deftly slipped aside, as Csizmadia's second charge slammed head-first into the wall. He shook his head, then charged Hitchcock a third time, twisting, kicking and head-butting while straining against the handcuffs, roaring like an animal "*Arrrrgh!*"

Sherman slipped his twenty-four-inch fiberglass baton under the chain between the handcuffs, placed the tip on the middle of Csizmadia's back and lifted up. The excruciating pain penetrated his fog of rage and alcohol, forcing him to bend forward. Hitchcock helped Sherman turn him around so he was facing the door. Csizmadia's chest began heaving. He inhaled and exhaled in loud gasps. His knees wobbled. He started to buckle.

"Don't buy it, Tom. He's faking. Don't let up on him," Hitchcock urged as he put his hand under Sherman's baton and the two of them lifted up until Csizmadia screamed.

The three staggered together through the narrow door. Csizmadia threw his body against Sherman, almost knocking him down, then Hitchcock. Crashing against the walls as they fought their way down the hall, Csizmadia collapsed at the head of the stairs. "Please, boys, I no go out my house," he said between gasps. As one man, Hitchcock and Sherman grabbed Csizmadia by the elbows and dragged him down the stairs, and out the front door.

Csizmadia's wife burst into tears and the children began screaming. When he saw his terrified family with the attendants from Flintoff's, Csizmadia got to his feet and tried to charge the men who were treating his wife's injuries. Hitchcock and Sherman stopped him. Csizmadia began kicking and spitting everywhere. He cursed in English and Hungarian the men who were treating the injuries of his wife and trying to calm the children for the trip to the hospital.

"I weel keel you all, your wives and children too for taking my family! Yeh! You wait till I out jail. I find you! I burn your houses down! I keel your dogs and cats too!" Lajos bellowed, his mouth spraying saliva at the cowering two attendants who came to aid and take the family to the hospital.

Neighbors came out of their houses. Csizmadia screamed "Help me! Help! The police, they beat me up!" as Hitchcock and Sherman fought him all the way to Sherman's cruiser.

"My God! Police brutality! Take your filthy hands off him!" shouted a neighbor woman. A man, apparently the woman's husband, got in Hitchcock's face. "Stop! Stop it right now! What is the meaning of this, officers? Why are you treating Mr. Lajos so horribly?" he demanded.

Hitchcock and Sherman ignored the neighbors as they struggled to cram Csizmadia into the back seat of

Sherman's cruiser. A tall slender man appearing be in his mid-thirties stepped in and tried to free Csizmadia, Hitchcock grabbed him by the front of his shirt, jerked him aside and stuck his forefinger in his face. "You've got two choices: Butt out, or go to jail for Interfering with a Police Officer. Pick one."

The man stared at Hitchcock, open-mouthed with shock as he stepped back. "Well, I never–" he said, his mouth still open, his heart pounding under his shirt. "I want your badge number," he said.

Hitchcock ignored him as he helped Sherman fight Csizmadia into the back seat, kicking and screaming. The hearse left with the family. The neighbor woman ran after Hitchcock, shouting, "Go to hell Pig! Pig! Pig!" as he left, following Sherman.

AT THE STATION, Sherman backed his cruiser into the prisoner loading bay. Hitchcock helped him drag Csizmadia out of the back seat, kicking and screaming in Hungarian, they fought him up the steps.

Lieutenant Bostwick, who had never made an arrest in his seven year career, was in the hallway when Hitchcock and Sherman prisoner burst through the station door. Trembling, Bostwick hid behind the coffee vending machine in an alcove as Csizmadia grunted, snorted, bellowed, kicked and threw himself into Hitchcock, then Sherman, crashing into the sheetrock walls of the hallway until they wrestled him into an empty holding cell and removed the handcuffs.

CATCHING THEIR BREATH, they brushed off their scuffed, disheveled uniforms and returned to their patrol cars.

"Some people you got in District Five, Tom! I'm changing my mind about buying a house there," Hitchcock said good-naturedly.

Sherman chuckled. "Actually, I have it on good authority that those folks were rednecks visiting from Eastgate!"

Hitchcock grinned. "If they were Eastgate people, they would've handled the Hungarian Gorilla themselves, and we'd never hear about it."

Hitchcock checked his Timex. 9:30 p.m. He was only ninety minutes into his shift. "We'd better get back on the street, Tom."

DISPATCH HAD ANOTHER call waiting when they called themselves back in service: *"Both units check the status of Three Zero Eight and Three Zero Seven at a fight involving a crowd of minors at the dance at Lake Hills Roller Rink, NE 8th and 164th Avenue. Neither has come back on the air in ten minutes, no one is answering the phone at the rink. Code Two."*

"Three Zero Six and Three Zero Five are en route Code Two, Radio." Hitchcock flipped his overhead light on and sped the three-mile straightaway of NE 8th to the call, Sherman following.

A crowd of over twenty teenagers milled around the dirt parking lot when they arrived. Two boys sat on the hood of a black-and-white patrol car. Neither Walker nor Otis were to be seen.

Hitchcock keyed his radio mic. "Both units arrived at Lake Hills Dance, got a large crowd of juvies in the parking lot. Patrol cars are here, no officers visible. I'll be out of the car, Three Zero Five will guard our units."

Teenagers began hurling the standard insults. "Hey look, more pigs are here!"

"Oink! Oink!"

"I smell bacon!"

He shoved one kid off the hood of the patrol car so hard he ended up sprawling on the gravel. The other kid hopped off in a hurry. He turned to a tall skinny kid in a gray sweatshirt with SAMMAMISH TRACK printed in red letters on the front.

"What's going on here, and where are the two officers?" Hitchcock asked.

"Butt out, piggy," the kid sneered, showing off for his snickering friends.

Hitchcock grabbed him by his shirt and jerked him up close. He reeked of beer. "You're drunk, sonny. If you're here when I come back, I'll arrest you for minor in consumption and take you straight to the Youth Center downtown, where the really tough kids will teach you a lesson. Now, where are the officers?"

He tightened his grip on the kid's sweatshirt, twisting it until the fabric squeezed the kid. "Uh–in-inside," the kid stammered.

"What happened?" he demanded.

The kid gulped. "Th-there was a big fight, a big fight, when someone threw pennies and trash at the singer. The pi–I mean the two cops b-broke it up. They c-closed the place."

Hitchcock released him with a shove. "Go home, sonny, and don't pee your pants as you leave."

He pushed his way through the jeering crowd to the dance hall. The hardwood floor that served as a roller-skating surface during week and a dance floor on Friday and Saturday nights, and the stage were littered with trash. The smells of sweat, cigarette smoke and soda pop hung in the stagnant air. Except for Walker and Otis in the middle of the dance floor with three handcuffed young male prisoners, talking to the manager and another employee, the place was empty.

"We're okay," Otis said. "We're taking these three in for assault, minor in consumption, disorderly conduct. They started a small riot by throwing trash and coins at the singer on the stage. A girl in the crowd climbed on the stage and attacked the singer, Jerry Lee Lewis, who threw her off the stage. That started everybody fighting. This one," Otis said, pointing at the tallest and strongest-built kid, "has assault warrants for him. The other two thought we wouldn't be able to arrest them. Help us get them through the crowd outside."

Hitchcock stared at Otis in disbelief. "You're putting me on! You mean *the* Jerry Lee Lewis, the "Great Balls of Fire" singer was here?"

"Yup, but he left. Let's get these punks to the station."

Baton in one hand, a prisoner in the other, each of the officers pushed and jabbed his way through the jeering crowd to their cars. Otis cursed when he found his front tires had been slashed. "I'll stand by for the tow truck," Sherman told Otis.

To keep the fighters apart, two went to the station in Walker's car, Hitchcock took the third prisoner, a minor, drunk, and in a fighting mood.

"Take these cuffs off and fight me, pig bastards," he told Hitchcock at the station, on the way to the booking room.

"Forget it, kid. I have calls waiting."

"You can't put me in the same cell with these two pukes you arrested me with," the kid sneered. "I'll just finish what I started."

Hitchcock checked the other cell, where Lajos Csizmadia slept on the only bunk bed. *He seems like a pretty good kid. Just needs a lesson in respect,* he decided.

"Kid, when you were little, did your folks take you to see Santa Claus?" he asked with a straight face.

Surprised by the question, the kid replied, "Yeah,

so?"

"Well, with your being so much tougher than the other two, I've got no choice but to put you in the other cell with one of Santa's helpers. He's old now, and he thinks he *is* Santa. When he wakes up, if you ask him, he'll tell you stories of the North Pole," Hitchcock told the kid as he put him in the cell.

Csizmadia was snoring. The kid shook him roughly. "Get up, old man, get up! I want the bunk and I wanna hear about the North Pole."

Hitchcock waited out of sight around the corner in the booking room where Walker was fingerprinting one of the prisoners. Seconds later, he heard Csizmadia.

"*Rrraaaughh!* So, you t'ink I tell you stories, eh? You want th' bunk, eh? I weel show you, pipe-squeak, who I really am. And what you really are!" The sounds of mayhem followed as the kid tried to resist Csizmadia.

"*Heellp! Helllp!* Officer, Please!" The kid cried out.

Walker gave his prisoner to the booking officer and went with Hitchcock into the cell area. Csizmadia had the blubbering youngster in a headlock, crushing him slowly like a human boa constrictor. The kid's face started turning blue from lack of oxygen. Walker, the former heavyweight state champion college wrestler, entered the cell.

"Let go of him, Lajos," Walker said, his tone calm and confident.

Csizmadia growled and shook his head as he kept

crushing the kid, whose arms began flapping like a bird.

Walker gripped Csizmadia's right arm above the elbow. His thumb pressed the nerve under the tricep muscle. Hitchcock yanked the kid out of the cell when Csizmadia released him.

Then the enraged Hungarian grunted and turned on Walker. Walker threw a full Nelson hold on him and held him until he yielded by nodding and saying in a weak voice, "Okay, okay."

Walker knew better than to trust Csizmadia. He maintained the hold until Csizmadia began to buckle. He collapsed when Walker released him.

Shaking and gasping, the kid pleaded, "Put me in the other cell! I'll behave. I promise."

"Did I hear you say 'please'?" Hitchcock asked sternly.

"Please!"

"Please what?"

"Please, officer, sir! Don't let that guy near me!"

Hitchcock put the kid in the same cell with the other two he had been arrested with. "The booking officer will get to you boys as soon as possible. No fighting. The one who causes trouble gets moved into Santa's cell," he warned.

MINUTES LATER, HITCHCOCK returned to his patrol car and radioed Dispatch he was back in service. Right away he got another call.

"Respond Code Three to a two-car fatality accident on 148th SE at SE 30th. The coroner and Flintoff's have been called and the accident investigation units are on the way."

He arrived at the scene to find a mangled red Camaro, its convertible top down, on the sidewalk of the southbound lanes of 148th SE. A young man in his twenties sat in the driver seat, leaning forward, hands at his sides, the top plate of his skull was missing as if it had been removed with a power saw, exposing his bright red brain.

He scanned the immediate area. Firemen from nearby Fire Station #2 directed traffic and set out flares. Another patrol officer attended to an injured and hysterical man a few yards away. His car, a yellow Corvette, was wrapped around a metal light pole in the median.

Witnesses told Hitchcock they saw him drag racing with the driver who died. Hitchcock heard the injured man tell the firemen the dead man was his brother. He protected the scene and identified witnesses until the traffic division and the coroner's investigator arrived.

THERE HAD BEEN no time to patrol his district all night. Calls kept pouring in from all over town: family fights, parking lot disturbances, in-progress car prowls, drunk driver arrests, loud music complaints, juvenile drinking parties. No one had time to eat, and Hitchcock's stomach growled. At the moment, he was the only unit not out on a call.

He called out at Charlie's Place, where Debbie the winsome blonde bar maid flashed her big blue eyes at him. "You look like a hungry man, Roger!"

He looked at her in surprise. "How did you know?"

Debbie smiled. "It's obvious—and late. All I got is a cold left-over leg of fried chicken."

"Just what I was thinking of!"

"What time are you off tonight?" she asked invitingly.

"The way the night's been, Debbie, maybe never."

He was munching the drumstick in his car to be near the radio, when, sure enough, Dispatch called again: *"Radio to Three Zero Six?"*

He let out a sigh of exasperation. *Don't these people ever sleep?* He wiped his hands with a napkin before he took the mic. "Three Zero Six, go."

"What's your 10-20?"

What now? "Just clearing a bar check at Charlie's."

"Respond to a prowler-in-progress in District Five. 12678 SE Twenty-Ninth. Woman and young daughter reports seeing a naked male adult in her back yard. Suspect climbed over the fence into her neighbor's yard. No units available to back you up."

"I'm almost there. Keep her on the line until I arrive." He tossed the drumstick out the window. Two minutes later he arrived in the same neighborhood where he and Sherman arrested Csizmadia a few hours earlier. He shut off his headlights as he neared the address.

"Three Zero Six arrived," he whispered into his mic. "Ask the woman to meet me at her front door in thirty seconds."

Taking his baton and flashlight, he opened the door of his cruiser, stepped out and eased it closed until he heard it click. An eerie quiet permeated the neighborhood as he hoofed it to the house under moonlight bright enough to read fine print. He rapped softly on the front door.

"Who's there?" a woman's voice inside asked.

"Police officer."

A frightened middle-aged woman with her hair in curlers opened the door with one hand, a blue steel revolver in the other, finger on the trigger, pointed at the floor. Hitchcock lifted his chin, inquiring.

"I just saw a totally naked man standing outside my bedroom window," she said, shaking.

"What did he look like?"

"Uh–like any buck-naked man, I guess!" she replied, flustered.

"Was he young or old, white, brown or black, tall or short?"

"Oh," she said. "Tall, six feet, maybe. Ball cap over gray hair, looks like Eddie Albert, the guy on the *Green Acres* TV show. When he saw I had a gun, he climbed over the fence into my neighbor's back yard. They're out for the evening. I heard their little dog bark, then it squealed. Now it's quiet over there."

"All right, I'll check it out, ma'am. Stay inside, please."

He laughed at himself as he went to the house next door. *Of the dumb questions I've asked on this job, that one takes 'em all. As if there's lots of naked guys roaming the streets at night!*

The house was dark inside. He slipped through the backyard and walked to the back. The lifeless body of a small white dog was lying on the patio by the sliding glass door, its body warm to the touch.

A faint tapping noise in the yard next door drew his attention. He peeked over the fence. A naked man stood on the patio, knocking on the sliding glass door. Keeping his eyes on the prowler, Hitchcock didn't say a word as he vaulted over the fence.

The prowler dashed across the yard to the next fence and scaled it like a gymnast.

"Stop! Police! You're under arrest!"

The suspect paused at the top of the fence to glance at Hitchcock, then dropped to the other side and disappeared.

Hitchcock bolted across the yard, climbed the fence, and dropped into the next backyard as the naked stalker ran through a gate on the other side of the yard, then dashed into the street. Hitchcock pursued. The suspect turned left and lengthened his stride.

Despite the weight of his duty belt and boots, Hitchcock began to close the gap, his boots making slapping sounds on the asphalt. He came within a yard of the suspect and reached for his shoulder when he was out of breath and his legs turned to rubber. His lungs were on fire, his pace slowed. *Cursed cigarettes!*

The suspect began regaining his lead. Desperate, Hitchcock stopped, drew his baton, a heavy, twenty-four inch hunk of black fiberglass, with his left hand, transferred it to his right, took aim, and threw it at the suspect's legs.

The baton flew end-over-end through the air, hit the pavement and tumbled between the suspect's feet, causing him to fall into juniper bushes at the edge of a lawn. Hitchcock staggered toward him, gasping for air. The suspect started to get up; hurt, but barely winded.

Hitchcock stumbled and almost fell on the shrubs as he reached for the suspect's arm. The suspect was on his feet, but wobbling. There was no time to plant his feet for a punch. Off balance and desperate, Hitchcock fired a long overhand right cross, a sure knockout punch, at the tip of the suspect's jaw, but lack of sure footing caused him to hit the suspect's mouth instead.

The punch sent the prowler flying backward into the junipers. Hitchcock tripped on ground shrubbery and fell when he lunged forward to seize him. He tried to stand, but his legs would have none of it, and his lungs were heaving.

The predator staggered to his feet, shaken, bleeding from the mouth. He staggered away, holding his jaw. Moments later Hitchcock heard a car start up a block away and tires screech.

Hitchcock sat in the shrubs, dejected, panting, nauseated, hating himself for smoking, a habit he picked up in the Army. Within seconds the headlights of Sherman's patrol car were upon him. His uniform pants and shirt were torn. He began throwing up as Sherman approached.

"You okay?"

"I caught him," he replied between retches. "My punch was off target. I knocked him down, but I tripped and fell when I went to grab him and he escaped."

Sherman drove Hitchcock back to his car. Lights were on in the houses on both sides of the street, a few people stood outside, clutching bathrobes around them to keep warm.

"The neighbors woke up and are in an uproar over this," Sherman said. "I'll be busy here for I don't know how long."

Beat, nauseated and dejected, Hitchcock wrote a detailed report and made a pencil sketch of the suspect's face.

His mind raced as he cleared the scene, thinking, *this guy is out of control to be prowling buck naked. Nothing happens in a vacuum. He didn't just decide one day to prowl neighborhoods naked. He evolved into it. He can't stop. Good or bad, nothing stands still. He'll keep going until he assaults, rapes or kills somebody, unless we catch him.*

He cringed at the thought of the trail of future victims this predator would leave behind before something or someone stopped him.

CHAPTER TWO
Death of a Hit Man

Bellevue Police Station,
Monday, September 21, 1970

CAPTAIN OF DETECTIVES Dennis Holland arrived at his desk at 7:30 a.m., dressed as usual in a dark suit, starched white shirt with barrel cuffs, conservative necktie. At thirty-five he was at the peak of his career and still climbing, due in large part to the city's explosive growth brought on by a four-year program of annexation of unincorporated areas east, north and south.

Holland had been a solid, proactive patrol officer, but his niche was in investigative work. He studied trends in crime, especially the methods and characteristics of organized crime groups, and advancements in criminal forensics.

Early on, Holland recognized patterns of infiltration

of law-abiding communities by organized crime through acquisition of legitimate businesses to hide their illicit earnings.

The Wilcox case fulfilled his predictions that the city would someday experience executions by out of town hitmen. It silenced his critics on the Department but not the inner circle of scoffers around the city manager.

IN MINUTES, DETECTIVES from the King County Sheriff's Office, as well as two of his own detectives and his sergeant would be meeting to discuss the murder of professional hit man Colin Wilcox, the man Hitchcock arrested in Charlie's Place, a tavern in the City's Eastgate district.

Holland pondered the circumstances of the arrest, the evidence in his car, the mysterious posting of five-figure cash bail, followed by a gangland style execution. His years of predicting that out-of-state organized crime groups would move into the suburbs were fulfilled.

Through contacts he cultivated with other law enforcement agencies and the criminal underworld, he kept abreast of Seattle's equivalent of the mafia, a local family which owned horse and dog race tracks, pinball machines, strip clubs on Seattle's Skid Row, and laundered their millions into high-density apartment complexes.

The family members lived in upscale neighborhoods in Bellevue and its suburbs of Medina, Clyde Hill,

Hunts and Yarrow Points. Holland remembered the old saying that organized crime people don't dirty their own back yards. That held true in the past, but no longer. The area was changing at jet speed. New people, new groups, are moving in.

TO HOLLAND, THE Wilcox case marked the beginning of the end of Bellevue's small-town innocence. He knew that crime grows best in the fertile soil of a prosperous, naïve public. Criminal elements become established more easily when those in leadership dismiss incidents like Wilcox's execution as isolated incidents.

Passive leadership aside, Holland resolved to find out who hired Wilcox, what his mission was at Charlie's Place, who ordered his execution when he failed his mission, and who carried it out. He expected more information from this morning's meeting.

Besides exchanging information with county detectives, the officer who arrested Wilcox would be coming. After months of hearing about Hitchcock's arrests, exploits in the field, and reading his reports, he looked forward to meeting the young rookie – and asking questions.

HITCHCOCK'S RENTED CABANA on Wilburton Hill was only two minutes from the police station. He awoke when his alarm went off, thinking about the naked prowler who escaped from him last night. The angst he struggled with returned – if not for his smoking habit, he would have caught the naked predator and future victims would be spared the trauma of sexual assault and possible murder.

He got out of bed, emptied the pack of Winston cigarettes from his uniform shirt pocket, and flushed them down the toilet.

His thoughts turned to the detectives he would meet in less than an hour. He knew them only in passing. They were the envy of most patrol officers because they worked nine-to-five, Monday to Friday, weekends off, wore suits or sport jackets, had their own desks, phones, personalized business cards and unmarked cars—a lot of status for working cops. Not counting supervisors, there were only five detectives. Too few for the fastest growing city in the state.

He grumbled at the usual drab Northwest drizzle when he let Jamie, his German Shepherd-Siberian Husky dog outside. The weather was one of those build-a-fire-and-stay-inside-with-a-book days.

After reheated coffee, hastily scrambled eggs, and a shower, Hitchcock slipped into laundered blue jeans, brown harness boots and a new Pendleton wool shirt. He strapped his holstered off-duty snub-nose .38 Smith & Wesson on his belt and covered it with his black windbreaker. As he left, he took a moment to touch the photograph of himself as a boy alongside his father and Bill Chace at the opening of Chace's Pancake Corral, before he left.

He entered the detective office at 8:00 a.m. sharp. The secretary led him to a conference room where six men in suits and neckties sat. The tall, dark-haired man in a dark suit at the head of the table greeted him.

"Welcome, Roger. I'm glad to finally meet you. I'm Dennis Holland, the captain around here, and these are the detectives who served the search warrant on Wilcox's car, Joe Small and Larry Meyn," he said, gesturing to two men Hitchcock had passed many times in the hallway.

"And our division sergeant, Stan Jurgens," Holland continued. "Over here are King County Detective Captain Ned Stone and Detective Roy Thomas."

Hitchcock noticed notepads, thick stacks of reports and unsealed evidence envelopes on the conference table as he shook hands with everyone and sat down.

Captain Holland said, "Roger, we asked you here today to learn more about your arrest of Colin Wilcox. We've verified that Wilcox was an out-of-town professional hit man, a suspect in several murders between Spokane and Chicago. He was paroled from the big house at Walla Walla earlier this year, where he served time for manslaughter. Joe and Larry have been working on this ever since you arrested him last week."

Holland turned toward one of the detectives. "Go ahead, Joe."

Detective Joe Small resembled Joe Palooka, the

blond-haired boxer in the comic book series.

"The evidence we found in Wilcox's car indicates he was hired for a mission that somehow involved Charlie's Place," Small began. "We don't know yet what his mission was, but it must have been a hit because he had a Browning High-Power nine-millimeter pistol, the one that hold thirteen rounds, three loaded magazines, and a police scanner in his car, set to monitor our two radio frequencies."

Small looked at Hitchcock. "You aren't gonna like this next part, Roger."

"What?"

"Wilcox recorded the shift hours of the Patrol Division, the call signs, the dates and times and the order the Eastgate units on night shift made bar checks. He specifically mentioned you by name and your callsign. He noted the time you called in service, the time you called out of building searches, then what time you called out on a bar check at Charlie's. All that in a notebook. You were targeted"

Sunned, Hitchcock leaned back in his chair, staring at Small, too surprised to say anything.

"It's humiliating for all of us that Wilcox conducted surveillance at the station every night for about four weeks without even being noticed," Detective Small continued, "by the end of that time, he had reason to be certain no officer would be checking Charlie's on a weeknight until at least nine p.m."

Hitchcock dropped his gaze to the table. "So he knew my pattern, my call sign, even my name and I had no idea," he muttered.

Detective Small went on: "Wilcox also recorded the descriptions and plate numbers of officers' personal vehicles. He knew when they arrived for work, and when they left. He learned about us from the police scanner in his car."

"Wilcox is dead, so how can we find out what this was about?" Hitchcock asked. "Who would have hired him?"

Detective Meyn, a pale, thirtyish man of average build, dressed in a gray suit and tie as drab as himself, replied "We know none of that now, but whoever hired Wilcox has deep pockets."

"I'm only a rookie, but weeks of surveillance, laying low and planning tells me Wilcox was a key part of something big."

"No doubt," Meyn said, "receipts in Wilcox's car from The Great Wall indicate he ate there in the evening eight times over the four-week period," Meyn said. "Always paid cash. The Great Wall is the only Bellevue business we found receipts for. At least twice he went to Charlie's from The Great Wall, from that, it seems to us that people connected to The Great Wall brought him here from the other side of the state."

"Amazing that he kept receipts," Hitchcock said. "They could be used to track his movements."

"I beg to differ–a criminal who keeps expense records indicates a disciplined, thorough professional, not a common thug," Meyn said.

Hitchcock nodded, indicating he stood corrected, but said nothing.

"The time and money invested tells us the mission was of vital importance to whoever hired Wilcox, and apparently money was no object," Detective Small said. "Discovering who hired and funded him will disclose what the mission was–"

"Hold on," Hitchcock interrupted. "Wilcox had no wallet on him and only a few bucks in cash when we arrested him. So where did the money he was operating on come from?"

"We found a key for a safe deposit box at a bank in Issaquah in his car," Small answered. "We got a search warrant and found over three thousand dollars in small bills inside. Other receipts indicate he always stayed at Alpine Motel on Highway Ten, in Issaquah. We discovered two gaps of several days each between his stays there. Where he went during those times is unknown. We found receipts for the false beard and wig, from a shop on Skid Row in Seattle he purchased two days before you arrested him. The shop owner remembered him. Said he was picky about the colors of the beard and wig matching, and paid cash."

"What about the gun he had on him?" Hitchcock asked.

Detective Small turned to his sergeant, Stan Jurgens, who impressed Hitchcock as having been a man of the soil in his past, a farmer or a rancher. His hands, protruding from buttoned white shirt cuffs, were big, heavy-knuckled and gnarled. His medium sized, round-shouldered build under his suit also bespoke a previous life spent doing outdoor work.

"The State Patrol crime lab identified Wilcox's prints on the Browning Hi-Power," Jurgens said, "the loaded thirteen-round magazine in the gun, and the other magazine in the glove box, also loaded. Wilcox must have worn gloves to handle the ammunition because there were no prints on any of the cartridges in either of the magazines. The Feds traced the gun from the factory to a sporting goods store in Spokane in '67. The original owner sold it a year later. It changed hands several times and hasn't been reported stolen, so how Wilcox got it is for the Feds to figure out."

"So, Wilcox was murdered to silence him before any deals could be cut which would expose his purpose," Hitchcock concluded, his hands folded on the table.

"That's right. We looked for links between the only two businesses in our city he went to, Charlie's Place and The Great Wall," Jurgens said. "No connection between the owners, Wally Evans and Juju Kwan. Joe and I showed Wilcox's mug shot to Juju. She insists she never saw him in her place or anywhere else, which cannot be true. We talked to the waitresses and bartenders there. Same story. Since Juju's employees are all Asian immigrants, it could be they have a cultural fear of the police. We can't be sure."

"Or maybe they fear Juju," Hitchcock offered.

"Yeah, or maybe they're here illegally," Meyn said.

"There's an underground international network of human smuggling from Asia," Captain Holland said. "Not all of them are young women or children captured for the sex trade. There's also a market for slave labor in restaurants, slaughterhouses, meat packing plants, and the like. Often times, family members of the slaves are held hostage under threat of death."

"Here? In the U.S.?" Hitchcock asked, surprised.

Captain Holland's expression was blank as he nodded.

Detective Meyn checked his notes. "We spoke with Wally Evans, the owner of Charlie's, who made a point of telling us how much he appreciates you, Roger, but it was the same story. Evans said he believes he never saw or heard of Wilcox before the he came into his tavern the night before you arrested him."

"Wally said he *believes* he never saw Wilcox? What's that supposed to mean?" Hitchcock asked.

"I asked him that. Evans said it was possible Wilcox visited his bar when he wasn't working, or maybe he just didn't notice him."

Noticing Hitchcock's dismay, Small asked, "Hey, Roger, you still with us?"

"Yeah, I just feel stupid. Making my routine so predictable that I put unknown others at risk."

Small shook his head. "It's an imperfect world, and in police work, all's well that ends well. Think about what would have happened at Charlie's Place if you *hadn't* changed your routine by going there earlier than you usually do. Who knows how many people would have been hurt or killed? We want you in on this because you upset the plans of bad people and District Six is your beat."

"Am I at risk now?" Hitchcock asked, looking at Captain Holland.

"To answer your question," Holland said, "Two nights in a row, Wilcox goes to Charlie's right after he leaves The Great Wall. He's armed with a high-capacity pistol. The second time he goes there is just before eight o'clock, when he is sure that no officers are on the streets to respond to an emergency."

"Makes sense. Wilcox was a pro," Hitchcock remarked. "He impressed me as having done hard time."

"Right," Captain Holland said. "Wilcox thought, after watching you and listening to you on the radio, that he had about an hour to do his thing and escape on the freeway before you arrived. He knows from studying your routine that you would be away from your cruiser checking buildings at the start of your shift. So before you radioed yourself as in-service, Wilcox goes into Charlie's armed with a gun, a knife, wearing a disguise."

Holland paused, then continued. "You aborted Wilcox's plans when you and Walker arrived at Charlie's Place earlier than ever before. It caught him so off-guard that he made mistakes and ended up in jail. My guess is Wilcox wondered if someone, a competitor or an enemy of whoever hired Wilcox, knew of the plan and snitched him off to you. Those who hired him must have concluded that someone who knew of their plan told us."

"Basically, you're saying there is no way to know if I'm at risk or not," Hitchcock said.

"That is correct," Captain Holland replied. "We've investigated this case up to the time Wilcox's body was discovered outside the city in county jurisdiction. All evidence indicates Wilcox was murdered outside our town. It's a County case now, but what his mission was and who hired him affects us, so we're staying on the case, in cooperation with the Sheriff's Office. So now Captain Stone has a few questions for you."

Captain Stone, a twelve-year veteran of the King County Sheriff's Office, a tall, lanky, easy-going sort who looked as though he might have played basketball in college, had an air of professional detachment about him. He had made investigating organized crime his sub-specialty as he climbed the ranks, which enhanced his stature and reputation in the local law enforcement community.

"First off," Stone began, "the manner of Wilcox's death is out of character for our local organized crime groups, our home-grown crooks." He slid a stack of 8x10 photos of Wilcox's body across the table to Hitchcock.

Stone continued. "The area surrounding the scene indicates Wilcox walked, obviously under armed escort, to his execution, rather than being killed, then carried or dragged along a game trail to the secluded spot, which would require two or three strong men. The exact location of the body is next to a hiking trail, about forty yards from the road. The body wasn't visible from the road, due to trees and dense foliage. His hands were bound behind his back. He was shot once in the base of his skull with a .22. The coroner estimates death occurred about two weeks before the body was discovered, which would be almost right after his release from jail."

Captain Stone turned to the bald, short, stubby figure of a man with him, Detective Roy Thomas. Hitchcock felt a negative reaction to the detective's broad, pasty face and the way his thin gash of a mouth curled into a cruel smirk as he held up an enlarged photograph of Wilcox's face.

"As you can see, Wilcox deteriorated so badly from inclement weather and animal activity that he was unrecognizable," the detective said in a mocking tone. "The toxicology report states a detectable level of barbiturate was still present in the organs, indicating Wilcox was probably doped up when he went there with his executioners."

Hitchcock avoided looking at Detective Thomas as he studied the photos. Most of Wilcox's face had been devoured beyond recognition by wild animals, probably coyotes and raccoons.

"This style of execution is consistent with East Coast mobs," Captain Stone explained. "We think Wilcox was executed for failing his mission and to make sure he couldn't cut a deal with prosecutors."

"I was about to ask about that," Hitchcock said as he continued to study the photographs.

"Until now, home-grown organized crime figures in Seattle have been mild and peaceable compared to their counterparts in other parts of the country," Stone said. "They operate topless bars and peep shows on Skid Row in Seattle and launder the money through real estate investments like apartment complexes and downtown parking lots. They live quietly in suburbs like Bellevue and never dirty their own backyard. They don't leave a trail of dead bodies behind them. They understand and accept that they are being watched."

"Clearly what we're meeting about today doesn't fit the home-grown people you just described," Hitchcock said.

"Correct. The execution of Wilcox for failing his mission and to ensure his silence indicates out of state organized crime elements recognize the future growth potential here and have acquired interests they will kill to protect," Stone replied.

Hitchcock continued studying the photographs of Wilcox's death scene as he listened to Stone.

"What led you to alter your patrol routine and go to Charlie's Place first, that night." Stone inquired.

He hesitated, wondering how experienced detectives would react to his explanation if he answered truthfully. "I can't explain it," he finally said, "but I have a strange ability to sense danger before it happens. It kept me and the men on patrols with me alive the two years I was in 'Nam."

He noticed the detectives at the table exchanging doubtful glances with each other.

"Really? That's it?" Holland asked.

Hitchcock nodded. "Plus what Wally Evans told me about a strange guy he thought was casing his place the previous night. I knew the next day would be payday, which meant a lot of people would be at Charlies with cash. The next night I felt inner urging to go to Charlie's first. It was so strong that I asked Walker to go with me."

"What happened when you got there?"

"As Walker and I headed to the back door, a guy with a beard stepped out, spotted us and ran back inside. We ran in after him. The owner indicated non-verbally to me that he was hiding in the ladies' room. I figured we must have interrupted an armed robbery seconds before it was to go down."

He scanned the room. All of the detectives were staring at him. He could feel their skepticism.

"Continue, Roger," Captain Holland urged.

"We learned that just before we arrived, Wilcox somehow locked the front door from the inside, presumably to prevent anyone from escaping. I think he was in the process of locking the rear door when he saw us, and panicked."

Captain Stone nodded as he listened, then asked Hitchcock, "So, what are your conclusions now?"

"Based on the fact that the owner told me this was the second night in a row that Wilcox visited Charlie's, but disguised differently, I believe the motive was murder," he said. "I just don't know who the intended victim was or why."

The room was silent. He saw the detectives casting more questioning glances at each other. When they returned their attention to him, he continued, "Maybe someone in Wally's past has it in for him. Whether drugs are involved, I have no idea."

"Anything else, Roger?" Captain Holland asked.

Hitchcock paused and looked around the room. He saw open skepticism on the faces of the detectives of both agencies. *They don't believe me*, he thought.

He cleared his throat, then said, "Yes. Last week a biker from up in Granite Falls was involved in an accident on I-90 just seconds after I saw him leaving the back of The Great Wall, which had been closed all night. I helped the state trooper arrest him. Later that night the trooper told me the biker's blood tested positive for cocaine which the biker said he got at a Chinese place here. I assumed he got the drugs at The Great Wall because it is the only Chinese place in Eastgate."

"Juju Kwan is certainly a suspect in this," Captain Stone affirmed. "And no doubt, the people behind Wilcox are aware of you, because you upset their plans. They'll suspect someone in the know tipped you off."

Hitchcock stared at Captain Stone, many questions racing through his mind.

"Although cops who nail bad guys by the rules are rarely targeted for retribution," Stone continued, "because of your sudden change in routine, the people who hired Wilcox will conclude you're a dirty cop, either in league with a traitor in their organization, or you're employed by a rival group. So, it could be that you're fair game in their eyes. Since we don't know who is behind this, you need to have eyes in the back of your head."

Hitchcock had heard enough. He stood up to leave and was about to announce his opinion when Captain Stone made a final comment.

"One more thing, Roger. In the process of investigation, we learned that Wallace Evans, the owner of Charlie's Place, did hard time in federal prison for fraud and embezzlement. A federal charge of racketeering for the Chicago mob was dropped. He was paroled in sixty-seven, came out here in sixty-eight. He and a partner named Louis Adragna, also an ex-con, bought the tavern with cash. Where the cash came from is a mystery. Adragna disappeared a year later and is still missing two years later. So we have two mysteries."

For long seconds Hitchcock stared in shock at Captain Stone, then at Captain Holland. "This is worse than I thought," he snorted. "For doing my job effectively, this is what I get, suspected of being a dirty cop."

"Not us, Roger, the people who hired Wilcox," Holland responded.

Feeling defensive and disappointed, Hitchcock looked at the other detectives at the table. "I see that you're all thinking the same thing," he said. "it's written all over your faces. Before I quit, if I do, I want to take a polygraph to clear my name." At that he walked out.

CHAPTER THREE
Buckwheats, Bacon, and a Spy

HITCHCOCK LEFT THE meeting, angry that none of the detectives believed he had a sixth sense for trouble about to happen. He stormed out, ignoring the greetings of other officers he passed in the hallway. Returning to his El Camino in the library parking lot, he sat, discouraged and musing.

He had overestimated himself and underestimated what and whoever he was up against. Wilcox surveilling him *at the station* for weeks without his knowledge proved it and brutalized his self-esteem. For all he knew, Wilcox had followed him around off-duty too.

He believed the detectives' warning that the people behind Wilcox would assume from his timely arrest that he's a dirty cop in the employ of a competitor. *What other conclusion could the people who hired, then killed Wilcox come to? But my fellow cops?*

He shook his head at the scope of the mess he'd gotten himself into. No doubt his explanation for changing his routine seemed far-fetched, enough that the detectives who warned him that he wasn't safe also wondered about his honesty.

It troubled him that the detectives missed the most troubling point about Wilcox: In spite of being armed and wearing a disguise, his motive wasn't robbery, at least in the ordinary sense. The extensive planning, the pistol with a high magazine capacity, weeks of surveillance of the police, switching disguises, his mysterious bail-out, followed by his almost immediate execution, indicated much higher stakes than robbing a small crowd of working people at a tavern on payday were on the line.

He'd misread Wally Evans, the jolly owner of a neighborhood tavern, the family man who told only clean jokes, who in reality was a convicted felon, a mob man, from Chicago, no less. That, as much as anything else, shook Hitchcock up, yet it explained how Wally recognized Wilcox as a convict. *Takes one to know one,* he thought.

The detectives, and Wally, too, must think I'm one dumb rookie. Maybe I'm not cut out for police work. Maybe I should quit and return to medical school. Like it was when Otis and I were kids, becoming a cop was another of his ideas that I fell for. Best not to let Joel pick my women for me, he mentally mumbled.

Sitting in his El Camino, oblivious to the damp cold, musing on his newfound devastation, watching people park near him, carrying books into the library, others come out, holding books in their arms, he finally inserted his key in the ignition. The small block 350 V8 fired up at the first turn of the key. He tuned the radio to KVI, 570 on the dial and left the station. It had been months since his schedule permitted him to listen to "Robert E. Lee" Hardwick in the morning.

Ahead of the Hardwick show was the local news, announcing a coalition of college students organizing in Seattle to protest the spreading of the war into Cambodia and Laos. In no mood to hear about the shenanigans of spoiled kids fearing the draft, he turned the radio off. His mind was swirling too much to pay attention to his driving—he just drove. Minutes later he found himself parked in front of the Pancake Corral. Thinking *at least here I'll be welcomed,* he headed for the door.

The welcoming aromas of bacon and eggs, fresh-brewed coffee, and pancakes soothed his bruised self-esteem when he walked through the door, mentally questioning his calling to be a cop. Lovely dark-haired Ada, one of the owners' daughters, seated him and brought him a steaming mug of coffee. "Allie will be right here," she said in a knowing tone of voice.

As he poured creamer into his coffee, the musical lilt of a woman's voice behind him cooed, "Morning, Roger.

53

Are you on a change of schedule?" He turned. Allie stood there, order pad in her hand. Her feminine aura, personal warmth, and woman scent erased a stressful morning of upsetting news and embarrassment.

"Just for today, Allie," he said, relieved by the refreshing effect her presence had on him. "How's your little one?"

"Baby teeth are coming in," she sighed. "Costing his mama her sleep." She checked her watch. "Four more hours before I can go home, and hopefully take a nap. What can I get you?"

"Buckwheat pancakes, a side of bacon, and a small slice of time with you when you're off."

She laid a hand on her hips and took a step closer to him. "That's it? No eggs? Just buckwheats, bacon and...? No dancing girls to entertain you while you wait until I'm off? Hmmm."

He smiled again, liking her sense of humor.

"No dancers today, just the morning paper and a little time to talk with you later."

She took up an abandoned *Seattle Times* and the morning *Seattle Post Intelligencer* and handed them to him. The *Times* featured a photo of a group of ratty-looking UW student protestors holding a sign that read: STUDENT POWER END THE WAR.

He put the *Times* aside and opened the sports section of the PI to Royal Brougham's column about the UW Huskies' Rose Bowl prospects.

He peeked over the top of the paper to watch Allie. Tired as she was, she moved efficiently, cheering up even the grumpiest customers, checking on orders, refilling their coffee, calling many by name.

The more he observed Allie, the more he discovered about her. A woman of the rarest order. As poor as her car suggested, she never complained. And attractive as she was, she avoided dating to give her full attention to her infant son. A rarity – a beautiful woman with integrity and without guile.

She brought his order and a note that read: *See you at Nick's on Park Row at 2:15.*

He ate quickly. She met him at the cash register. "Okay. Nick's, it is, but before that, I need to borrow your car," he said.

Stunned, she stepped back. "What? Why?"

"Police business. Today only. I need another car they won't recognize me in," he fibbed.

"When will you bring it back?"

"In about two hours, I promise."

She squinted suspiciously up at him. "This sure is unusual of you, Roger Hitchcock. What's going on?"

"Can't say yet, but I'd appreciate your helping me out." He held out his hand. "The key?"

She left and came back with the key. "Two hours, period. Gray Toyota parked in the back. I'm holding you to it."

*How I wish you would hold me to it. I'm available ,*was

his instant thought. "Don't worry, I'll be back in time."

Allie's Corolla was a sturdy little beater in need of some TLC but it started with the slightest turn of the key. At his first stop he withdrew cash from his savings at the downtown National Bank of Commerce. He noticed a man sitting in a gray Oldsmobile when he came out of the bank.

He noticed the same man watching him from a distance when he had new tires put on Allie's car at the Firestone Tire store across the street. Then, at Barney and Al's Chevron, a stone's throw from the Corral, an oil change and tune-up, he spotted the same man in the gray Oldsmobile as he filled Allie's gas tank. *This guy's way too old to be Allie's ex—maybe he's after me,* he thought as he checked his Timex. 1:50 p.m.

Feeling good and anxious to see Allie's response, Hitchcock strolled back inside the Pancake Corral, handed her the key, said thanks and left.

He helped himself to a cup of coffee and took a seat facing the door and the window at Nick's BBQ, a long, narrow diner set at the end of Park Row, a one-story strip of shops that faced 104th Avenue, the main drag through Bellevue's downtown. It had the ambience of a cafeteria; linoleum floor, Formica-topped tables set in Naugahyde-covered booths, but the quality of the food more than made up for it.

At 2:15 Nick's was devoid of customers except for Hitchcock. He watched Nick, the wiry Italian middle-age owner, working the oven behind the counter, preparing beef roast for the upcoming dinner crowd.

Allie came in, blue ski parka over her waitress uniform, an expression of dismay on her face. He got to his feet. "Roger! You didn't have to do that! Why did you?"

"It's your honorability."

"Honora-what?"

"Honorability."

"Whatever. I can't accept this. I can't afford to pay you back!"

"No strings attached."

She stared at him, probably trying to figure out what he was up to, spending a lot of money on her without asking her out. *Yeah, with SO many eligible women after him, he doesn't need to attach strings to anything or anyone. No chance for a single mom like me. He probably did this out of pity and nothing else.* "Nobody's ever done anything like this for me before. I mean, really. I–"

He interrupted her by ordering Nick's specialty, ground ham hamburgers with fries and another coffee for her. "Tell me about your situation; how it happened..."

She hesitated, then shrugged her shoulders as she began. "I'm from a working-class family. I met Glendon, my son's father, when I was a freshman on a scholarship in accounting at the UW, working as a coffee shop waitress at the downtown Frederick & Nelson store.

After a month of dating, I told him I was pregnant."

"How did he take the news?"

She blushed and lowered her gaze. "The first thing he said was 'So who's the lucky father?'"

"Glendon sounds like he needs a lesson in manners. What did you do?"

"I slapped his face and reminded him I was a virgin when we met."

He visualized the scene, impressed by her pluckiness. "Then what happened?"

"He insisted on an abortion. I refused. He agreed to marry me only in a civil ceremony. He hates Christianity. His parents disapproved of me when they found out. Under their pressure he filed for divorce less than three months later."

"You went through pregnancy and childbirth, alone. As a divorced woman?"

She bit her lower lip and looked away.

"Glendon's a real waste of skin, isn't he?"

She gave a quick grin at his comment. "My family supported me, but you can imagine the damage he did to my reputation. Two years later his parents took me to court for full custody of Trevor. They hadn't seen him even once. Glendon never saw him until after he was a year old."

"You've got custody. What happened in court?"

"He and his parents lied about me, but the judge, God bless him, didn't accept anything they said; he all but called them liars. I got full custody, child support and maintenance. Glendon got limited visitation."

"Hooray for the judge. So why didn't his parents like you?"

"My background, I guess. A construction worker's daughter. Dad died of a heart attack four years ago. My mom's a Safeway cashier. We're Renton people. Too blue-collar for rich folks like them. They were ashamed of me."

He mulled over her situation as they ate in silence. As he finished first, pushed his plate aside and got up to refill their coffees, he spotted the same gray Oldsmobile parked across the street, facing them. *Is that guy out to hit me, or is he following Allie?* he wondered again.

"My turn to wait on you, for a change," he said in a kidding tone as he refilled her coffee.

"Being the curious type that I am," he said as he sat down again, keeping an eye on the Oldsmobile across the street. "I decided to see what your ex looks like so I watched him leave your place after our first meeting at the bank parking lot. The new Benz he drove didn't match his sloppy appearance, so I ran the plate. You can really pick 'em, Allie. McAuliffe. One of Washington's oldest families, and the richest. Vast holdings in timber, real estate, banking, and politics. Two past governors, and a state senator in the family line. They own big chunks of downtown Seattle."

"I knew nothing of his family until after we were

married," she said, finishing her sandwich.

"Rumors have it that Horace McAuliffe, your ex-father-in-law, is a communist sympathizer who secretly funds radical groups and anti-war activists. Did you know about that?"

"I'm not political," she said, shaking her head. "The only thing Glendon told me about his parents after we were married was that they maintain underworld connections."

"Like what?"

She shrugged. "Mafia stuff, I guess. He told me once his parents have made people disappear."

"Sounds like Glendon read *The Godfather*."

She scoffed. "A reader he's not. He never talked politics with me. He made the comment only once, in passing, no details, so I don't think he was bragging or making it up."

"What else happened?"

"Glendon never took me anywhere. I didn't fit in with hoity-toity people and never will. He's never worked–lives on an allowance from his parents which they threatened to cut off if he didn't divorce me."

Hitchcock marveled at her as she talked. Pure class. Movie star level looks and a figure to match, yet it hadn't gone to her head. *With her beauty and smarts she could write her own ticket in life, but instead she's a humble waitress, struggling to do right by her infant son. The rat who fathered her child doesn't deserve her.*

60

"How are things are working out for you since the court fight?"

She scoffed again. "The court based the amount of child support on what Glendon's parents, through their attorney, said Glendon's monthly trust allotment was. They all lied. So what I receive is pitifully small. He punishes me by always being late and making excuses."

Keeping an eye on the man in the gray Oldsmobile watching them from across the street, he said, "Topic change. What about this Jim Reynolds guy you told me about at our first meeting? Any more from him?"

"He called last weekend. Wanted to meet for coffee but I turned him down. Told him my son had the sniffles. Before I could end the call, he went off on another of his tirades about using violence to right the wrongs in this evil country of ours."

"I want you to tell me every time he calls you. Right away," he instructed. "And don't agree to meet him again. Make excuses. I haven't figured out yet who he is, or what he's up to." He handed her a slip of paper. "My phone numbers. Home and work."

He avoided looking at the man across the street as he walked her to her car. She cranked the window down. "Thank you so much for helping me, Roger. It means a lot to have a friend like you."

"We'll stay in touch," he said, then went back inside Nick's, where seconds later he saw the gray sedan cross the street and head in the same direction Allie took.

He sprinted to his El Camino in time to follow the gray Oldsmobile as it followed Allie to her apartment.

An overweight, middle-age man, wearing a lived-in brown sweater and baggy green corduroy pants, slipped out of the Oldsmobile, holding a camera to his face. The man crept, bent over, among parked cars in the apartment parking lot, knelt behind a parked sedan and began snapping pictures of Allie as she ascended the stairs to her apartment.

Hitchcock eased out of his El Camino and snuck up on him from behind. "Hey, you. What're you doing?"

The sudden challenge startled the spy. "Uh, nothing, really. Who's asking?"

"I am. Say, nice camera! Pentax Spotmatic, eh?" Hitchcock snatched it from the man's hand, cranked the film winder until it stopped, opened the back, pocketed the film roll, and handed the camera back

"Hey! What the–what do you think you're doing?"

"Wrong question. What are *you* doing hiding in the bushes, following and taking pictures of the young woman as she went up those stairs?"

The spy's face reddened. "None of your business. Give me the film back and I won't call the police."

He flashed his badge. "I *am* the police. We have an ordinance in this town called vagrancy, defined as wandering and prowling without a legitimate purpose, which is exactly what you're doing. You have two choices. One–explain yourself. If your purpose is legit,

I'll return your film. Or choice two–refuse to explain yourself, I take you in and impound your car. Pick one."

The man's shoulders drooped as he sighed. "Okay, officer. I'm a private investigator. Licensed in Seattle. I have that woman under surveillance for a client." He produced his wallet, then held his credentials out to Hitchcock. The license, issued to Tobias Olson by the City of Seattle, was current.

"Now give me my film back."

"Not so fast. You could be just saying that. Maybe you're not Tobias Olson. Maybe you're a stalker. What other ID you got?"

The man sighed again and peeled out his driver's license. "Satisfied now, officer?"

Hitchcock hesitated. "You could still be somebody else. Washington driver's licenses don't have photographs."

The man flapped his arms at his sides, turned his head to the sky and grunted in frustration.

"Who's your client and why is the woman under surveillance?" Hitchcock asked.

"My client's identity is confidential. You oughta know that. Now give me that film!"

"No dice," he said, making eye contact with the man. "With so many young women being stalked these days by men your age, I'll write up a report and forward it to my supervisor. He'll refer it to the City Prosecutor to decide if charges should be filed. Of course, before your film is released, in addition to knowing who your client is, they'll have to determine if you're licensed to conduct business in the City of Bellevue. If not, you'll be charged with conducting business here without a license. So, are you?"

The frumpy PI grimaced and cursed as he got into his car. "You'll hear from my attorney about this, and you can go to hell, officer!"

"Been there already. Twice."

As the private spy drove away, Hitchcock pondered the roll of film. *Why would a private dick be spying on a poor waitress, a single mom like Allie? Dark secrets? Blackmail?* He shook his head. *Can't be. Not her. No way.*

The feeling that he was being watched came over him. He glanced around until he spotted a petite, middle-aged blonde woman with a blue scarf over her head standing at the bottom of the apartment staircase, watching him. She had a striking resemblance to Allie.

He acknowledged her with a slight nod, which she returned. *Must be Allie's mom. She must have seen me confront Olson. Bet she knows what's going on.*

HITCHCOCK WENT TO the City Photo Lab and gave Frank Kilmer the film and the story. "I'll have it ready in a couple days," he promised. "Got two deadlines to meet first."

He headed home, meditating on the day's events. Police detectives telling him his life could be at risk after his arrest of Wilcox, learning of Wally Evans's hidden criminal history, his Chicago mob connections, and the strange disappearance of his partner in crime and business, a private detective following Allie, and a mysterious radical showing her his gun and constantly calling her.

Exhaustion came over him as he entered his cabana. The need he felt to lie down surprised him. *I got off work early last night for the meeting this morning. I have to work at eight tonight,* he remembered. He set out food and water for Jamie, laid out his uniform and gear on the couch, and set his alarm to go off in three hours. As he stretched out on his bed, he sensed that the shift to come would bring change.

CHAPTER FOUR
The Reaper's Man

8:00 P.M.
Four hours later

DISPATCH HAD A call for Hitchcock the second he radioed himself in-service: *"See the manager at the Cedar Grove Apartments, 1510 140th SE regarding a D.O.A. Victim's parents are standing by. A detective has been called, the coroner is on the way. Code One."*

The rain and the traffic were light as he acknowledged, thinking, *Yeah-yeah, Code One, victim's dead, just another stiff, so what's the hurry, right?* He set his windshield wipers on intermittent and rolled out of the station parking lot.

He'd been to this low-income apartment complex several times on domestic violence, underage drinking, and car prowl calls so many times that he and Greg, the manager, were on a first name basis.

The shortest route to the scene was the scenic one. From the station, he turned right on 116th and followed it under the Wilburton Trestle, the last wooden train trestle in the state after which it became the Lake Hills Connector, a divided four lane road recently punched through one of Bellevue's largest green belts. Swampland at the bottom, but a lush forest of alder, cedar, maple and birch trees, dense growths of ferns, brush and grasses on the hillside. He remembered Blacktail deer once lived here before the new road was punched through, before he went off to war. *They're long gone now, driven out by the traffic and noise. Only scavengers–rats, racoons and coyotes are left,* he mused.

The Connector topped out at 140th Avenue SE. A left turn at the signal and two blocks down on the right brought him to The Cedar Grove Apartments. He checked his Timex as he called out. 8:12 p.m.

Hitchcock found Greg, a gaunt retired schoolteacher with thinning black hair slicked straight back, fidgeting and pacing outside his office, smoking a cigarette.

"You rang?"

"Thanks for coming so quickly, Roger," Greg said, too stressed out to respond to a humorous greeting.

"What's going on?"

Greg hesitated. Hitchcock, seeing his distress, waited. "This young girl, Janine, was renting Unit Eleven, upstairs for about three months," Greg began. "She's–she *was* a student at Bellevue Community

College. Her parents pay her rent. When they stopped hearing from her, they drove up from Olympia. The door was locked. So I let them in..." Greg stopped, the words stuck in his throat, unable to finish.

"Take your time, friend," Hitchcock told him gently. "Tell me the rest when you're ready."

Long seconds passed. "Is life really this ugly, Roger?" Greg finally asked, his voice cracking, tears filling his eyes. He shook his head and removed a white handkerchief from his back pocket.

Hitchcock paused, then asked, "Are you okay enough to take me to the parents?"

Greg sighed and wiped his eyes with his handkerchief and nodded. "Follow me."

In the rental office, he introduced Hitchcock to a grief-stricken couple appearing to be in their early fifties, both dressed in sweaters and overcoats. He followed them to Unit 11, where the stench of decaying flesh pierced their eyes and nostrils. On the carpeted living room floor in the sparsely furnished one-bedroom apartment was the naked body of a slightly overweight young white female, lying supine, legs spread wide apart, a hypodermic needle on the carpet inches from her vagina.

Purplish blotches of advanced postmortem lividity were evident on the lower parts of her body, indicating death had occurred in this position. Old needle marks were visible on the inside of her left arm, multiple fresh needle marks were at the edge of her vagina. Rigor mortis had passed. The thermostat in the hall read sixty-six degrees. Based on the room temperature, his training and experience as an Army combat medic, Hitchcock estimated death occurred two days ago.

The victim's mother handed Hitchcock a white piece of paper. "We found this lying next to her."

The unfinished letter was from the victim to a man named Willie in which she expressed in the crudest terms the sexual favors she would bestow on him when he got out of the state penitentiary at Walla Walla.

The father became agitated. "I'm going outside to check for Janine's car. Maybe there's something in it that will help this officer find out what happened to our daughter," he said.

"I'm very sorry for your loss, ma'am," Hitchcock said after her husband left. "I appreciate this is very hard for you and your husband. If you are up to it, please tell me everything about your daughter, starting with who her friends were."

The mother stared at the floor, shaking her head slowly as she wrestled with the ugly reality in front of her, doing her best to hold her grief in check.

"We're a Christian family. Janine is...was...the youngest of our four kids. Always the wild one, the family rebel. At home in Olympia, she rejected our principles, always got poor grades, avoided church, ran away from home to be with the wrong crowd. In her early teens, she experimented with drugs and had sex with older boys. First it was marijuana, later she got into LSD through that rotten, terrible college professor who should be shot."

The husband returned. "Janine's car is gone," he told Hitchcock.

"I'll write up a stolen report. You sign it. We'll take it from there."

He logged the time he sealed the apartment door with evidence tape, parked his cruiser at the bottom of the exterior staircase and keyed his radio mic: "Three Zero Six, Radio, request permission to broadcast stolen car information."

"*Proceed, Three Zero Six,*" Dispatch replied.

"To all units—we have a signed stolen report on a green 1969 Ford Maverick four-door, bearing Washington license Ocean Paul Adam Six Three Seven. Vehicle has a crumpled left front fender."

A HALF HOUR passed. The victim's parents had gone home. Hitchcock greeted Ian Barstow, the county coroner's investigator, known to cops for his Canadian accent, sentences punctuated with "Ay," and his quick, gallows wit. Barstow had a dead body on a gurney in the back of his station wagon. Seeing a man's hand dangled below the green cover sheet reminded Hitchcock of black-and-white horror movies of the fifties.

Detective Small arrived. Hitchcock led him and Barstow upstairs and removed the yellow crime scene tape and logged the time of their entry of the scene in his notebook.

The manager was closing up when Hitchcock returned to the rental office. "Tell me about this girl, Greg. Who her friends or visitors were, what kind of people were they, and what happened to her car?"

Greg looked as if he felt responsible. "Her car is gone, eh?" He said, shaking his head. He took a deep breath and exhaled loudly. "I *should've* called you, Roger, but I hesitated. I thought the activity I saw was suspicious, but the black guy... If it turned out to be nothing, people would label me a racist. Now I wish I had called instead of being such a coward."

"What black guy?" Hitchcock pressed in. "What made you suspicious?"

"This black guy. Always coming to Janine's apartment, always bringing different men with him."

"He's black. How else would you describe him?"

Greg paused for a moment. "About forty. Never saw him outside of a car, so his height and weight I can't say. Dark skin but not real dark. He didn't seem to be heavy-set or thin."

"What kind of car did he drive?"

"An older model white Lincoln. Sometimes a white girl with short blonde hair drove for him. Other times I saw Janine leave in her car – a green Maverick – and come back, followed by one or more men in another car–" Greg stopped as though the enormity of what he said just hit him.

"Go on," Hitchcock urged.

"Then, day before yesterday," Greg continued, his voice shaking, "the black guy came here with the blonde girl in the white Lincoln. A half-hour later, I saw the blonde leave by herself in the Lincoln. A few minutes after that I saw the black guy drive away in Janine's green Maverick. He was by himself. Today the girl's parents showed up. Wish I had called," Greg said, ruefully shaking his head. "Didn't want folks thinkin' I'm prejudiced. Still, I shoulda called."

Woulda-coulda-shoulda, Hitchcock thought as he wrote out the statement from Greg and had him sign it.

He returned to the scene and handed Greg's statement to Detective Small. "The dad signed a stolen report on the Ford Maverick. I already called in the description to all units. But now I need to add the suspect description."

"Yeah. Call in the suspect description, Roger, then come back. We'll need your help."

Upon receiving clearance from Dispatch, Hitchcock keyed his mic. "All units, witness reports seeing the green Ford Maverick leaving the Cedar Grove Apartments about forty-eight hours ago, driven by an unidentified negro male adult, older looking. The driver is a suspect in the DOA case at this complex. Consider armed and dangerous."

He returned to the apartment. "We gotta get this guy, Roger. Barstow says this is his second heroin overdose death in Bellevue tonight," Small told him.

"Second? When was the first?"

"A couple hours ago. Meyn got called out on that one."

"Same guy involved?" Hitchcock asked.

Small nodded. "Looks that way. Don't know for sure yet. Meyn's still at the scene."

"Hey, Hitchcock," Barstow said. "Give me a hand getting this girl onto the gurney and downstairs."

He glanced at Small, who was gathering carpet samples with tweezers and placing them in small evidence envelopes. "Don't look at me, Roger," he chuckled. "I've got neighbors in the complex to interview after I'm done here. Besides, tradition says the rookie at the scene always helps move the stiff."

"Ha-ha," Hitchcock muttered. Barstow spread out a green cotton sheet on the floor next to the body. "You get the heavy end, the upper body. Don't worry, I got her feet," Barstow snickered.

Hitchcock grabbed the two corners of the sheet closest to the victim's head. Barstow took the other two corners of the sheet and made eye contact with Hitchcock. "Ready? One-two-three—up we go."

The smell of decaying flesh nauseated Hitchcock. Even Barstow, who picks up dead bodies every day, turned his head when they lifted the body off the floor by the sheet underneath it.

"Don't drop her. The skin's ready to burst," Barstow cautioned. They placed Janine on the gurney in one motion and strapped her down. Hitchcock's eyes watered from the stench as he held onto the heavy end of the gurney. For a moment he flashed back to recovering dead soldiers from the battlefields of Southeast Asia as Barstow guided the gurney to the bottom of the stairs and slid it into the back of his station wagon.

"Heroin's spreading into the suburbs now; two dead in your town tonight, ay," Barstow said in his crisp Canadian accent as he closed the rear door of his wagon. "This new stuff from Vietnam is so potent most addicts can't handle it. Many of 'em are dying. You should see what it's like in Seattle."

HE CLEARED THE scene and headed for the Hilltop Inn, next to Highway 10, a hangout for pimps, prostitutes and drug dealers, hoping to find the stolen green Maverick there. It wasn't. He began calling in the license plates numbers of cars in the parking lot to Records. on the local law enforcement database for stolen property and outstanding warrants.

He got a hit on a white '65 Cadillac Fleetwood for armed robbery and unlawful possession of a firearm for the registered owner: Ronald Davis, NMA, DOB 7-8-45, height six-feet-two, weight one-eighty.

"Received. Confirm the warrant while I switch back to F1." Hitchcock keyed his mic. "Three Zero Six, Radio, I'm sitting on an unoccupied vehicle parked at the Hilltop Inn with active felony warrants for the owner. I'm waiting for Records to confirm. Requesting backup. I'll be on F2."

He got out of his cruiser, glanced all around for anyone watching him, then shone his flashlight into the interior. It was empty. Nothing on the seats. The hood felt warm to the touch. He parked his cruiser at a distance, observing the Cadillac, and waited for the driver to come out.

The radio began crackling, then, *"Records to Three Zero Six, switch to F1 for a call."*

He switched back to F1. The dispatcher's voice said *"Check out reports of a woman screaming for help, area of 149th and SE 14th. We've had three calls so far; unknown situation. No backup units available. Code Two."*

Arriving in the neighborhood in four minutes, he spotted a middle-aged man in a gray sweater and khaki pants on the street, waving to him to pull over.

"I'm the one who called. There's a woman screaming somewhere up there, around the corner," he said, pointing uphill. "Sounds like she's saying something about her son."

A woman's wailing cut the air. "There it is again," the man said, his eyes on Hitchcock. "If it involves the oldest of the Fowler boys, it'll be bad."

Hitchcock drove up another block and rounded the corner. He recognized the fortyish woman on the street in a worn gingham dress. It was Barbara Fowler, the mother of a childhood friend, shouting for help, waving her arms in frantic motion. *This has got to be about Randy*, he thought as he drove up to her and got out of his cruiser.

"Thank God it's you, Roger!" she exclaimed. "Randy's overdosed. I think he's dead!"

"Where is he?"

"In the house! Quick!"

He bailed out of his cruiser and ran with Barbara into the run-down little rambler.

"Why didn't you call us from your house, Mrs. Fowler? It would've saved time."

"The phone company turned off the service yesterday. My check bounced," she said through her panting and sobbing.

Hitchcock dashed into the cluttered living room, where his childhood friend laid on the couch, Eyes closed. Bluish skin cool to the touch. Hitchcock pressed his fingertips into Randy's neck. No pulse. He dragged Randy to the floor by the front of his shirt. "Start your heart, Randy!" he commanded as he began chest compressions and mouth-to-mouth resuscitation.

Barbara Fowler stood by, wringing her hands, crying and praying "Oh God, save my son! Jesus, save my son. *Please!*" she pleaded over and over.

After two minutes of frantic CPR efforts, Randy began coughing.

Hitchcock rolled him to his side. Randy spit up phlegm and mucus on the carpet.

He scooped his emaciated friend into his arms and carried him to his patrol car. "Quick, Mrs. Fowler, open that door and get in the back. We're going to the ER. We've no time to lose!"

He laid Randy on the back seat and settled his head on his mother's lap, closed the door and hurried to the driver seat. He fired up his cruiser, flipped on the overhead emergency light and keyed the radio mic.

"Three Zero Six, Radio, leaving the scene. I revived the victim and am transporting him with his mother to the Overlake ER. Code Three. Advise the ER to be standing by."

"Radio to Three Zero Six, you do not want Flintoff's for the transport, correct?"

"Affirmative. Victim not breathing, no pulse when I arrived. I gave him CPR. He's breathing now but we can't wait."

"Received. We will notify Overlake ER."

He flipped the switch for the siren and weaved around traffic through intersections, west on Lake Hills Boulevard, north on 148th Avenue, hitting speeds of seventy, and eighty, with frequent braking and breath-taking lane-changes through traffic on the way to the straight three-mile stretch of NE 8th to the ER.

Violent convulsions seized Randy. His spasms crushed his mother into the seat as she held him and shrieked raw, plaintive pleadings that cut Hitchcock to the heart. "Don't die, son! Don't die!" She sobbed. "Please! Oh God, don't let Randy die, please, please, *please!*"

The volume of Barbara's desperate pleading with the Almighty for her son's life overrode the wailing siren as Randy retched, spasmed, coughed and vomited on her lap.

"I'm getting us there as quickly as I can. Keep talking to him!" Hitchcock shouted to her over the siren.

Cars heading in both directions pulled over as the black-and-white cruiser with red light and siren in full operation, reached speeds of seventy, eighty, and over ninety on the open, flat stretches of NE 8th Street, slowed for hills and sounded long blasts of the siren before he busted red signals at intersections as fasted as he dared.

He came to a screeching halt in front of a nurse and two orderlies waiting at the curb under the metal canopy at the ER entrance. Hitchcock opened the rear door. Randy had turned blue again. The hospital team laid him on a gurney and whisked him inside, his despairing mother following behind, unmindful of her son's vomit on her dress.

Hitchcock followed as the orderlies wheeled Randy into the Intensive Care Unit and closed the doors, leaving Barbara outside in the hallway.

"Randy's safe now, Mrs. Fowler," Hitchcock said. "We got him here alive, and what happens next is out of our hands. Maybe now you can tell me what happened. Let's step into this waiting room where we can talk."

Barbara's face darkened. "I'm gonna tell you everything, Roger." She looked at him and hesitated. "I've got so many fond memories of you and Randy in Little League when your dad was the coach," she said. "You two were friends but Randy wasn't like you. He couldn't stay out of trouble. Always went with whatever wind was blowing. Got into the hippie thing when it came out, which led to pot."

"I didn't know any of this, Mrs. Fowler," he said.

"Of course not. You were over there, defending the country. Anyway, Randy dropped out of school, got into cocaine and anything else he could get high on. We all thought we had his habit under control until he met a pusher last spring, that black bastard from Seattle, who got him hooked on heroin."

"Tell me about that," Hitchcock said.

Barbara nodded bitterly as tears filled her eyes. "Randy, who couldn't keep a job, suddenly had money all the time, yet no work. Wouldn't tell me where it came from, but I knew. From the money he couldn't explain, to the needle marks on his arm, and how much weight he was losing, it was obvious. Now this. I have a gun, Roger, and when I see Tyrone again, I'll shoot him till he drops dead."

"You said his name is Tyrone? Tell me about him."

Barbara wiped her tears again. "He's colored and I hate his guts. I know you had negro friends from your boxing days, but...forgive me, I'm an angry and bitter mom. Tyrone Guyon is his name. He's in his forties. A pusher and a pimp. He offered Randy free heroin if he got my daughter Connie hooked. You can guess what he wanted her for. He threatened me when I stepped in and stopped it."

"How did he threaten you?"

"He pointed a pistol at my head, in my own house, in front of my kids. Said he'd kill me. But *I* didn't back down. *He* did. I called his bluff. He's a coward," Barbara said, sniffling. "So today, I saw him give Randy some of this new heroin he says is from Vietnam. Today he shot it into Randy here, in my house! Right in front of me! Randy collapsed. I started screaming. He was blue. Tyrone left in a hurry. Thank God a neighbor called the police. Then you showed up and knew what to do. We owe you for saving him, Roger. I guess you knew what to do because you were a medic in the Army."

Doing his best to keep her focused, Hitchcock asked "Mrs. Fowler, how can I find Tyrone? Where does he live?"

"I don't know. Randy can probably tell you. Tyrone always shows up unannounced."

"*How* does he show up? In a car, with someone, or

what?"

"Always in a big white Lincoln, not new. The one I saw him in today is different, a small car. A fairly new Ford...a Maverick, I think."

"Is that car green?" Hitchcock asked.

She looked at him in surprise. "Why, yes, it is. A young white girl drove it. Chunky. Short blonde hair. She reminded me of Mae West, the slut in the movies. Tyrone was passenger. Do you know Tyrone?"

"Not yet."

A short, balding, middle-aged man wearing hospital scrubs with a face mask and a stethoscope dangling from his neck entered the room.

"Mrs. Fowler?" he asked. Barbara nodded. "I'm Dr. Collier. Randy is out of danger for now. He's very lucky to be alive. We've stabilized his heart rate, sedated him, and put IVs in him to keep him hydrated. We'll keep him under observation for twenty-four to forty-eight hours. He'll need treatment after his release. A case worker will come in to ask you for information about his medical history, including his drug use history."

After the case worker met with Barbara Fowler, she sat in the front seat as Hitchcock took her home. They rode in silence until they arrived. "Show me Randy's room, Mrs. Fowler,"

"I'll even help you search," she said.

In minutes he found a stash of five balloons filled with white powder, hypodermic needles, a burnt spoon, and a short length of surgical tubing in the nightstand next to Randy's bed.

"Look what I found in Randy's closet," Barbara said, holding a white envelope stuffed with ten, twenty and fifty-dollar bills, and a plastic baggie filled with what Hitchcock recognized as marijuana.

She knelt on the bedroom floor, crying and shaking her head. "I don't know what to do, Roger. This is destroying my family."

"Actually, you're in a position to help a lot, Mrs. Fowler," Hitchcock said as he packaged the drugs and cash in separate evidence envelopes.

"How?"

"Help me take Tyrone off the streets. Randy must know how to find him. Second, you can be my eyes and ears for others like Guyon. You can save lives like Randy's."

"Count me in," she said, nodding her affirmation. "Soon as my phone service is back on, I'll leave messages for you."

AT THE STATION, Hitchcock sealed the evidence in marked envelopes and locked them with state crime lab drug analysis request forms in the evidence room. He handed his report to Sergeant Breen.

"Nice work!" Breen exclaimed. "You've not only gotten a lead on who our bad guy is, you literally saved a life tonight. Keep up this kind of work and you'll be taking my job before you know it."

"Nah, I like it right where I am. I'm having too much fun. Babysitting would ruin it."

Breen chuckled as he said, "Ran a check on Tyrone Guyon. He's got an out-standing felony warrant for illegal firearm possession. His rap sheet includes drug-related offenses, weapons charges and promoting prostitution, all occurring in Seattle."

Hitchcock nodded. "Guyon's here a lot and we've gotta find him. He's selling a new strain of heroin from Vietnam that's stronger than the usual stuff on the streets. We had two deaths from it tonight, and almost a third. The coroner's investigator told me addicts in Seattle are dying from it. Also, Guyon was apparently the pimp of the second victim. He was seen driving her car by two witnesses about the time of her death."

"Good work," Breen said. "I confirmed the warrant in case any of our guys see him. Mugshots for our bulletins are on the way from Seattle PD. Get back on the street. Almost everyone is out on a call."

OFFICERS WERE GASSING up their cruisers before turning in, but Hitchcock returned to the Hilltop Inn, hoping to find either the Cadillac with warrants on it still there, or Tyrone Guyon in his white Lincoln or the green Maverick.

No such luck.

He headed to the gas barn, remembering his

childhood years with Randy. *How different we've become,* he thought, grieving. *Despite his father being the town drunk, Randy had been a good kid, a pal. Look at him now, an addict and a pusher who ought to be in jail.*

While the gas tank of his cruiser was filling, Hitchcock opened the back door. He saw mucus and phlegm on the floor and the seat where Randy had been.

As he wiped the mess up with paper towels, Tyrone Guyon came to mind. *Three heroin overdose cases in one night. Two dead, one barely survived. Guyon is the common thread between two, and possibly three. He overdosed Randy in front of his mother indicating he killed Janine in the same manner. The totality of the circumstances ought to make enough probable cause for us to arrest Guyon for investigation of homicide. Are any of the detectives looking at the overdoses as murders?*

With drug arrests and overdoses on the rise, it mystified him that the Department didn't have a narcotics unit. According to Otis and Walker, the city manager's office clamped down on earlier efforts to create such a unit. No reason given, which told him something was wrong somewhere at the top, while innocent citizens are paying the price.

For now, he thought, *I'll concentrate on putting Guyon where he belongs, in the slammer. He's got a warrant out for him. I'll arrest him on thar if nothing else when I find him. He's probably armed. Randy will tell me.*

CHAPTER FIVE
From Tacoma With Love

WEDNESDAY WAS FRIDAY for Hitchcock. His gut instinct told him to visit the bar at the Wagon Wheel first thing. The same attractive barmaid who made eyes at him a few nights ago was there. She appeared to be in her early to mid-twenties, neck-length dark brown hair, fair skin. Medium height, slim, and buxom. She possessed an easy-going friendliness and seemed modest and genuine. Beyond her physical attributes, he only knew her name was Gayle. He assumed she was single from her bare ring finger.

Just before 2:00 a.m. he returned, helped her lock up, and escorted her to her car, a white '68 Dodge Dart.

"I'm off for the next couple days," he said.

She looked up at him and smiled. "Me too."

"Could I interest you in dinner out of town,

maybe?"

"You could, maybe."

"Six-thirty tomorrow?"

"Yes. Know where I live?"

"Nope."

She flashed her eyes at him. "Just up the hill, by the college. Follow me."

He followed her to the apartment complex at the college entrance and walked her to the door.

"I'll be needin' your phone number," he said, wearing a boyish grin.

Dark eyes looked up and locked into his. "Let me have your pen and that little notepad in your shirt pocket."

"Help yourself," he said daringly.

She stepped closer, reached into his shirt pocket, wrote her name and number on the pad, then tucked it back into his pocket and patted it. She gave him a quick smile and went inside her apartment.

AFTER BREAKFAST AT Brenner Brothers Bakery, a trip to the cleaners, and a workout at the Iron Works gym, he took his El Camino through the car wash on Auto Row, shined his shoes, dressed, splashed on a little English Leather cologne. He arrived at Gayle's apartment on time.

Strong seductive appeal shone through her modest dark, knee-length skirt, off-white blouse with lace on the front and black lambskin leather jacket, which perfectly coordinated with her hair and ivory complexion.

For covert reasons, he took her to The Keg, a steakhouse located miles north of Bellevue in Bothell, where there would be no risk of being recognized, and its deep, high-back booths allowed for confidential conversation. He ordered whiskey, she a glass of white wine. As soon as the waitress brought their drinks and left, Gayle laid her cards on the table.

"I don't know if you know anything about me," she said. "But I want to tell you that I'm a former junkie."

Hitchcock shifted in his seat, trying to hide the shock that hit him like a punch between the eyes. She came across too wholesome and healthy to be a former junkie.

He cleared his throat and ruffled the cloth napkin in his lap. *Welcome to the world, Ozzie,* he mentally told himself. "I'd like to hear about that, if you don't mind," he said.

She leaned forward, hands on the table, a brief, slight smile came and went "I don't mind," was her calm reply. "My brother Tony and I were raised by our grandmother in Tacoma after our parents died in a car accident. We were teenagers. Tony was two years older than me. Growing up. he was always in trouble. He got into drugs after our parents died. It was pot at first, then pills, then heroin. Since we were close, I did what he did. I got addicted and ran with the same crowd as Tony until he died right in front of me from an overdose. It was hard, but I was so scared I quit, cold turkey."

She paused and studied Hitchcock to gauge his reaction.

Sensing she was watching for signs of judgment on his part, he made a point of appearing calm and understanding.

"Right after that I came here to start a new life," she continued. "And, in case you're wondering, I've never been arrested. Check me out if you haven't already. I won't be offended."

He paused to take a sip of his whiskey. He was intrigued by both her history and her honesty. "What else? High school? Married? Kids?"

She shook her head as she smoothed the cloth napkin in her lap. "None of the above. I was seventeen and getting good grades when I dropped out in my senior year after our grandma died. I've never been married, no kids. I did some modeling for local department and clothing stores, but quit when future work was on condition of other demands. Tacoma is a tough town."

They were interrupted by the return of the waitress. He ordered ribeye steak, medium rare, with baked potato, loaded. Prime rib, well done, au jus and mashed was her choice.

He felt foolish for not checking her background, which even she thought he should have done, given the fact that she was a barmaid, new in town, no ties to anyone. The notion of running criminal records checks on girls he dated was a foreign concept to him. Since she startled him with facts about herself he'd never have guessed, he resolved to check later to see if there was anything else she hadn't told him, even though her candor made him feel confident of her truthfulness.

Now came his turn to step up to the plate. He described his family, boxing, the sudden death of his father, his decision to quit college and enlist, mentioning little of Vietnam and nothing of his old flame, Ruby.

The waitress reappeared with their orders. The savory smells led him to order another round of the same drinks to go with the food. They ate in silence.

"Where I work, we heard about you making that arrest at Charlie's," she said. "What a scary deal that must have been. I'm sure it had something to do with it being payday for nearly every business around."

"It's still under investigation."

"The owner and the manager at the Wagon Wheel don't like you guys checking on them all the time," she said, "but after the arrest at Charlie's and the big fight you were in downtown last month, they don't make critical comments anymore. And you ought to know, they may not like you or want you coming around, but now at least, they respect you."

Hitchcock snickered.

"What's funny?"

"When I was in the police academy," he said, "one of the first things our instructor asked us was, "Who in this class wants to be liked by the public when you arrive at the scene of a call?" There were twenty-five of us and about four guys raised their hand. Our instructor told them, "You boys should turn in your badges right now and get jobs as firemen. Everybody loves it when the fire department shows up. Never us."

Gayle chuckled. "I never thought of it that way."

"What about the other bars in Eastgate?"

"I'm new here, but there's the lounge at the Hilltop. A lot of dopers go there. Hookers too, from what I hear. White drug dealers drink at the Wagon Wheel. Blacks go only to the Hilltop. Our place is too red-necky for them. The bar owners all know each other, except for the Chinese joint near Charlie's."

Hitchcock pretended casual interest as he asked, "Oh? You mean The Great Wall? What about it?"

"No one seems to know much. From what I hear, only Orientals from Chinatown go there. If our customers go anywhere else at all, it'd be Charlie's or the Steak Out. Maybe once in a while the Blue Dolphin, that little lounge on the other side of the freeway. I rarely hear anything about the Chinese place."

"Want to help me do some good?" he asked.

"Sure. What?"

She accepted his offer of modest pay to inform on criminal activity in Eastgate. He knew he was on dangerous ground. Gayle was a beauty. He regretted there could be no romance.

"The three deadly sins that destroy cops are bucks, broads and booze," Sergeant Baxter told him during his first night on duty, based on a guess that Hitchcock's weakness is women. As his field training officer, Walker pounded it into him again and again during his one-year probation.

To be effective in fighting the drug epidemic, he needed informants, ones he could trust, who have street savvy.

The evening lasted long. The later the hour, the more Gayle gave up useful tidbits. Names, places, rumors, inside information that had no meaning to her, but the familiar names and details opened his eyes about the drugs, hookers and armed men who often stopped by for a drink, a meal, for drugs or sex on their way through Eastgate.

By evening's end, Hitchcock had a new perspective on his beat, and his first informant. He realized Gayle had only divulged part of her story. Knowing the rest wouldn't be hard.

They were quiet on the drive back to Bellevue. Gayle stood at her door, awaiting a goodnight kiss. He didn't hesitate long, being male and single. What could he do? He was surprised at how well she kissed. He kissed her again and wanted more, but stopped. It isn't supposed to work this way, at least not so soon.

HE STAYED UP long enough to write down what he had learned. In the morning he would make a copy for Sergeant Breen without naming her. The glimpse Gayle gave him about the criminal undercurrents that flowed through Eastgate with such subtle regularity that few officers were ever aware, led him to double the ammunition he expended in weekly practice with his service revolver.

The criminal history checks he ran on Gayle the next day checked out. Just as she said, she was clear of any criminal history, not even a traffic ticket; neither Tacoma PD nor the Pierce County Sheriff's Office had any record of her. He verified her identity through her driver's license and her Health Department permit, a state requirement to serve drinks or food at an establishment. Her story that her brother Tony died from heroin overdose also checked out. Lovely Gayle was legit.

He had his first informant. Based on her revelations about herself, he believed she would be effective. Better arrests, identification and interdiction of pushers and pimps, burglary rings and stick-up men were on the way. He felt good about having taken his first step in penetrating the underworld.

Paying Gayle with Department money would be a hard sell to Sergeant Breen. He decided to pay her from his own pocket if that's what it took to keep her. The biggest challenge would be supervising her without getting romantically involved. Gayle was alluring and attracted to him, and he to her. He grinned at the thought of police work now. Going back to medical school was off the table again.

CHAPTER SIX
The Cesspool

THE NEWEST BAR in town was The Trunk Lid, a dark dive located in District Four, the industrial zone in the geographic center of the city, on the four-lane Bel-Red Road. The former warehouse resembled a military bunker; concrete, low-ceilinged, its few windows were narrow horizontal slits a few inches below the ceiling. Even on a sunny day the structure emanated an ominous aura.

The two owners were of the new breed of entrepreneurs: smug white males sporting afro hairdos and handlebar mustaches, large-collared shirts, bell-bottom polyester pants, greedy opportunists who used and sold cocaine and pot and scorned authority.

They created a pseudo-funky atmosphere with scuffed, beat up, second-hand chairs and tables, a juke box, pool tables, a stage, sound system, and worn out, soiled sofas. The walls, ceiling and the floor consisted of dark gray, unfinished concrete.

For those who had grown up in west Bellevue, never knowing how "the other half" lived, going to the Trunk Lid amounted to a walk on the wild side. The coarse barmaids and their outlaw biker boyfriends, usually ex-cons who worked there part-time as bouncers, held a barbaric appeal to sheltered middle-class suburbanites, eager for an exciting break from their sterile cocoons.

Once the word got out that ID would be only winked at, kids in their late teens went in droves to The Trunk Lid to get drunk, get high and act up with adults.

MARK FORBES REPORTED for duty after recovering from his injuries at the Village Inn fight. He was assigned District Four, next to Joel Otis in District Seven, whose acceptance he craved to the point that he walked the way Otis walked, used the same expressions Otis used, and took up smoking cigars, as Otis did.

An hour into his shift, Forbes stopped a car for speeding on the road in front of The Trunk Lid. During the stop, a group of hecklers arrived and taunted him with obscenities as they walked inside. He recognized one of the males as an eighteen-year-old he arrested for disorderly conduct two months earlier.

Thinking the bravado of making an arrest by himself in a doper bar would redeem his reputation after being beaten so easily outside the Village Inn, Forbes keyed his radio mic. "Three Zero Four, Radio, clear the traffic stop. I'll be out on a bar check at The Trunk Lid. A minor I know just went inside. I'm going in to make the arrest."

The dispatcher replied: "*Received. Three Zero Four out at The Trunk Lid to make an arrest at 2116 hours. Will you be needing a backup?*"

Forbes, a body builder who had never been in so much as a shoving match before he was beaten to a pulp in the Village Inn fight, prepared for his return to work by increasing the amount of weight he lifted. Going in alone to make an arrest was his chance to prove himself and rebuild his reputation. He keyed his radio mic: "Negative, Radio. I can handle it."

Loud rock music blared all the way to the street through the closed doors, blasting Forbes in the face. He steeled himself and strode into a cultural jungle of danger and hostility on his quest to recover his manhood.

The bouncer at the door was an outlaw biker type; beard, ragged denim vest, prison tattoos on his huge arms and hands. It occurred to Forbes that maybe he should back out and wait for backup, but the thought of the "attaboys" his peers and his sergeant would give him for single-handedly facing down a crowd of hostile punks overrode his better judgment.

Like an omen, the music that came on as Forbes

threaded his way into the crowd was the latest protest song, *Four Dead in Ohio* by Crosby Stills, Nash and Young, released after the shooting deaths of four student protestors by Ohio National Guardsmen at Kent State University.

The sight of a lone, swaggering policeman riled the crowd whose inhibitions were lowered by alcohol and drug consumption, combined with the marching cadence of defiant lyrics, set the stage for what happened next.

Imagining himself as Dirty Harry in uniform, Forbes penetrated the crowd, pushing aside couples dancing to the music, as his eyes searched for the underage male he saw entering minutes ago. The crowd got ugly quick.

"Better watch who you shove, pig."

"Whatcha doin' here, pig?"

"Got no back-up, jack?"

"Gonna shoot us too? Looking for somebody to club, oinker bastard?"

Forbes, feeling a rush of excitement from his moment of macho derring-do, threw caution to the wind. He reveled in the insults and kept looking. By now he had penetrated deep into the crowd, far from the front door. He smelled marijuana smoke. Then it hit him. He had gone too far into a hostile crowd to be alone. He couldn't see the front door from where he was. The crowd's hostility was palpable, he was alone, and sur-rounded.

Somewhere along the wall a flame flared up. A tall, thin long-haired male sucked on a metal pipe, staring at Forbes with daring eyes. Fear chilled Forbes' limbs.

He realized he would have to fight his way out if he made an arrest. Then again, this was his chance to redeem himself after losing the first fight of his life so quickly. How humiliated he felt, lying helpless on the pavement with two other officers, then Hitchcock and Otis arrived and crushed Beecham and McMinn so fast they made it look easy.

Forbes's heart was in his throat, realizing too late his mistake in entering without backup. Too late now to back out. With something short of a death wish, Forbes moved deeper into the dark recesses. Another flame flared up in a far corner to his left. He smelled marijuana smoke stronger now. His eyes spotted a couple on a couch, puffing on a bong. They stared vacantly at Forbes, too stoned to react to even a police uniform.

He ignored the couple on the couch in order to continue his search for the minor he knew. He found him in the back, sitting on a sofa with two other young men, drinking beer, staring, mocking, blowing smoke at him as he approached, scoffing his presence.

"You're under arrest for minor-in-possession, Barry. Let's go," Forbes ordered.

Under the influences of alcohol and marijuana, Barry and company laughed in his face. "No way, man.

I ain't goin' anywhere with you," Barry said.

Alone and outnumbered, Forbes steeled himself and grabbed Barry by the arm and pulled him off the couch. "I said you're under arrest, and resisting arrest will be an additional charge."

He put an arm lock on Barry and reached for his handcuffs. The two other youths tried to pulled Barry away from Forbes.

"Off the pig!" someone yelled. Another youth threw a punch at Forbes, hitting him on the shoulder. Someone else kicked him in the butt. The defiant lyrics of *Four Dead in Ohio* stirred the crowd that now surrounded Forbes as he struggled to keep his prisoner.

Never had Forbes been so afraid. He stood alone in a darkened, noisy bar, surrounded by an angry, drunken crowd unimpressed with authority. Mild injury was the best he could hope for. He shoved his prisoner's friends back and snapped a handcuff on Barry's right wrist, pulled him close and said in his ear, "We're going out of here together, Barry, even if it's by ambulance."

The prisoner shouted to the crowd, "Hey, the pig just threatened me! Get him!" Two men from the crowd shoved Forbes from behind. On the brink of paralysis, Forbes tightened his grip on his prisoner.

The ruckus happened to get the attention of four off-duty Bellevue motorcycle officers in plain clothes on the other side of the bar. Sergeant Bill Harris and three of his men happened to stop by after post-shift training for a beer at the new bar before going home. Harris asked a barmaid, "What's going on over there?"

"Some stupid pig picked the wrong place to make an arrest. Looks like the crowd's gonna throw him out of here headfirst! I hope they do! You guys oughta go see it," she said, laughing.

"Yeah, we'll do just that," Harris said. He and his men left their beers and threaded their way through the crowd to the hecklers who were about to take Forbes down and free his prisoner. They barged in from behind, laughing and pretending to be confused drunks who didn't know whose side to be on, shoving the onlookers and yelling, "Hey, yeah, yeah, let's fight!"

In the free-for-all that followed, Forbes recognized his off-duty comrades. He clapped the other handcuff on his prisoner and used him as shield and battering ram to force his way through the crowd, and out the door to his patrol car where he belted Barry into the back seat.

On the verge of hyperventilating, Forbes keyed his mic: "Three Zero Four to Radio," he gasped. "Clearing a disturbance at The Trunk Lid. One in custody." In his haste to leave, Forbes forgot about the off-duty officers who saved him, never thinking they might need help.

"I want my phone call!" Barry shouted at Forbes in the booking room. "My dad will have your job for this, pig!"

"Cool your jets until we have time to get to you," Forbes said as he locked Barry in a holding cell.

LESS THAN AN hour later, a man in his late forties, Hawaiian suntan, pleated tan gabardine dress slacks, red silk shirt under a brown leather car-coat and reeking of alcohol appeared at the station front desk. "You're holding my son here. I came to take him home. Bring him out," he ordered the desk clerk.

Sergeant Breen met him. "Your son was arrested for being a minor in possession of alcohol in an adult drinking establishment. The officer recognized your son as a minor from a previous arrest. He arrested your son, who with several of his friends not only resisted the arrest, they assaulted the officer and your son attempted escape."

"This is ridiculous!" the father shouted. "Barry is a good boy. We'll settle this on Monday. I'll sign for my son. Bring him here."

Breen shook his head. "There are too many charges for that. Barry will go to jail and stay there until he goes before a judge, who will set bail Monday or Tuesday."

The father looked as though a vein in his forehead was about to pop. Before he started shouting again, Breen told him, "Barry was arrested for four offenses. Drinking alcohol in a public bar as a minor, resisting arrest, assaulting an officer and attempted escape. It's likely your son will be charged with a felony for assaulting a police officer, and attempted escape. It will be for a judge to decide."

The dad loudly scoffed at Sergeant Breen. "Apparently you don't know just who I am, Sergeant! Your Chief, John and I are good friends. We golf together! As a business owner in this town, I pay your salary. I can have your badge and the arresting officer's badge for this, just like *that*," he said, snapping his fingers. "Now let my son go. I'll be responsible for him. I don't want him exposed to criminal elements in jail."

Sergeant Breen leveled his stare at the father. "The charges are too many and too serious. No matter who you know or what you say, Barry goes downtown, and he stays there until a judge has time to see him."

"You'll be hearing from my attorney, Sergeant!" the father shouted.

"Tell your attorney I am Sergeant Jack Breen, and our chief's name is Sean, not John. Good night"

The father glared at Breen. "Now I see why the kids call you guys P.I.G. That's what you are!"

SERGEANT BREEN REALIZED citizen complaints against Forbes would be filed. After speaking with Sergeant Harris by phone, he brought Forbes into his office. "Tell me everything that happened there tonight, Mark," Breen ordered.

After listening to Forbes, Breen was alarmed at his recklessness. He set Forbes in an empty office to write a detailed report, while he called Captain Delstra at home. "Sorry to bother you so late, Erik, but something's come up that you should know about before we get any further into the weekend."

Delstra paused several seconds after Breen finished stating the facts. "At the very least, it was reckless of Forbes to enter a place he knew was filled with a hostile crowd to make an arrest by himself," Delstra said. "Think what would have happened if someone took his gun during the struggle and someone got shot or his gun was stolen from him. It bothers me that Forbes abandoned the four off duty traffic officers who saved him in the bar; he didn't even bother to tell anyone they were there and might need help. What if they were hurt?"

Breen took notes as he listened to Captain Delstra.

"The fact that no one from the bar tried to help Forbes or even called the station for help is grounds for an investigation that should result in the suspension or revocation of their business and liquor licenses," Delstra said.

"I'm thinking we should suspend their City business license at the very least," Breen said.

After a short pause, Delstra said, "What happened to Forbes is a challenge to our authority that must be met. Starting tomorrow night, bar checks at The Trunk Lid will be done by no less than four officers in helmets at least twice on Friday and Saturday nights. They are to check ID of anyone they suspect of being underage. They will arrest them, and any drug users they catch in the act. Anyone they arrest will be booked into the county jail. No one is to be cited and released. The officers will identify the bartender for later referral of charges for serving minors. Do not put Forbes on the team. Doing so would give the impression that the Department is out for revenge. Assign Forbes to the downtown beat and leave him there."

"Anyone in particular I should pick?" Breen asked.

"Otis and Hitchcock are to head the team, along with two others you pick," Delstra said. "You know the men on your squad. Pick two more who are *intentional* cops, like Otis and Hitchcock, who are here to be policemen, not to climb the ladder or do their first year twenty times over for the pay and the pension benefits. Have all reports ready for me on Monday. Keep me informed of anything else that happens, no matter how late it is."

BREEN THOUGHT ABOUT Delstra's instructions. He based his choice of Otis and Hitchcock on his knowledge of their personnel files and their decisive ending of the parking lot brawl at the Village Inn. They were hometown boys who grew up next door to each other. Both came from stable families, saw combat as Army medics in Vietnam, where they experienced killing.

Breen knew Otis was six years older than Hitchcock,

and served in Vietnam during the final days of President Eisenhower, when the Viet Cong were known as the Viet Minh. The secrecy of his service indicated he may have been on the find-and-kill missions, which targeted communist leaders. More than once before the fight at the Village Inn, Otis had demonstrated his skills with baton and bare-hand techniques.

Breen also knew that Otis convinced Hitchcock to join the Bellevue PD instead of Seattle. As curious as Breen was to know about Hitchcock's second tour in Vietnam, he knew better than to ask. His record for that time was sealed for a reason.

AFTER FORBES LEFT to take his prisoner to the county jail, Sergeant Breen drove to The Trunk Lid. He parked about forty yards away, shut down his engine and lights, and turned down the volume of his radio. His supervisor's car lacked the roof-mounted emergency red light and spotlight, so its profile would be less noticeable at a distance in the dark.

He rolled his window down to listen as small groups of long-haired young men, some hanging on their women, staggered outside, heading for their cars. Raucous laughter and cursing were carried on the night air. Breen could hear every word, as if they were within feet of him. Some sat in their vehicles in the dark for long minutes before they left. He decided to have LaPerle, the only officer not out on a call, meet him.

As he reached for his radio mic, LaPerle came on the air: *"Three Zero Three is en route to the station. One in custody."*

LaPerle was Breen's last available unit. A trip through The Lid would have to wait until tomorrow night.

CHAPTER SEVEN
Smackdown

Saturday - 2:00 P.M.

GAYLE CAME TO her door wearing a black leather jacket over a pale gray turtleneck cashmere sweater, and blue jeans which accentuated her good figure, and clog-style high-heeled shoes which added to her height. She smelled as fresh and clean as she appeared.

They headed east on Highway 10.

"Here's your first case," he said, keeping his eyes on the road as he handed her a folded slip of paper. "People are dying from this guy's heroin. It's from Vietnam, I'm told, and much stronger than regular heroin. He's also armed and wanted on felonies in Seattle. We want him on a death by overdose case and a stealing the victim's car last week."

Gayle read the note. "Tyrone...Tyrone...," she repeated the name, thinking. "Someone told me about a

Tyrone... It'll come to me." She paused for a few seconds. "Got it! This week I overheard one of our regular customers at the Wagon Wheel talking about a Tyrone who hangs out at the lounge at the Hilltop a lot."

"How does she know this?" he asked.

"She works there part time."

"What did she say about him?"

She shrugged. "What you'd expect—a pimp who sells heroin and cocaine."

"How often do you see this customer?"

"She comes in with her husband and another couple on Fridays after bowling. Saturdays she comes in late, and alone, so she must work then."

"What kind of work does she do there?"

"She's a nightshift maid."

"A *nightshift* maid?"

"She cleans bedrooms after people leave so they can be rented again."

"As in rooms rented by the hour?"

Gayle nodded. "That's why she works nights, Roger. She told me once I would be shocked to see who uses those rooms. Where're we going, by the way?"

"I happen to like Issaquah. Thought we would go there for a bite before I go to work."

She smiled contentedly. "Sounds good. Remember I work tonight too."

† † †

The Squad Room - 7:45 P.M.

SENSING A SHIFT was in the wind, the mood of the officers, Hitchcock included, was subdued. From the podium, Sergeant Breen scanned the eight men of his squad.

"Last night," he began, "a crowd at The Trunk Lid attacked Forbes when he tried to arrest a minor for drinking there," Breen said. "If it hadn't been for the intervention of Bill Harris and three motor officers who happened to be there off duty, Mark would've ended up in the hospital, or worse."

Hitchcock glanced to his left to see Forbes's reaction. Deadpan. He shook his head. *That's twice someone else has had to bail Forbes out of a fight,* he thought, remembering the Village Inn fight two months ago.

Sergeant Breen continued. "Captain Delstra has weighed in on this," he said. "The behavior of the crowd at The Trunk Lid amounted to a challenge to our authority, and tonight we're gonna meet the challenge."

A stir of excitement and approval wafted among the seated officers. "For the next week at least, bar-checks at The Trunk Lid will be done by no fewer than four officers at a time, in helmets."

He peeked over his shoulder at Forbes again. The malicious smirk on his face troubled Hitchcock.

Breen continued: "Here are the district assignment changes Captain Delstra wants for the next week: The Trunk Lid bar-check team will be headed by Otis and

Hitchcock, plus Walker and Sherman. Otis and Hitchcock will be a roving two-man unit, Three Zero Nine. Forbes will be in District Three, Sherman will take District Four, Allard in Six, LaPerle in Eight, Walker in Seven. Districts One and Two will keep your normal assignments. Diss-*missed!*"

Hitchcock watched in dismay as Forbes stormed out of the squad room, sullen and seething. He turned to Otis as he gathered his briefcase, baton, and helmet. "Some attitude Mark's got," he said.

"He's been humiliated again," Otis said. "Not only were there no kudos for bravery as he hoped, the Brass excluded him from participating in rousting the Trunk Lid. He feels he's being punished."

"Not sure I want to work with him after seeing this," Hitchcock said.

"Mark needs a reset," Otis said.

A LIGHT RAIN was falling when the squad of four met outside. Otis turned to Sherman. "Keep an eye on the place. Let us know when the parking lot is full and the music can be heard on the street, that's when we go in. We'll meet behind it, out of sight," he said. The other two nodded their agreement. "Also, Breen's instructed Dispatch to have other units handle our calls, so Ira, stay within a few blocks of the place so we can respond quick when Tom gives us the signal."

The rain stopped a half hour later while Hitchcock

and Otis patrolled the industrial area, never more than a few blocks from The Trunk Lid. They avoided traffic stops or anything else that might prevent them from responding to Sherman's alert.

Walker patrolled in the same loose manner, waiting. This was one night The Four wanted no calls, no matter the type.

Finally, at 10:00 p.m. Sherman came on the air: *"Three Zero Four to Three Zero Nine?"*

"Three Zero Nine, go."

"It's time."

The four-officer special detail met at the pre-arranged spot behind the bar, headlights off, out of view of the front parking lot. They gathered in front of Otis's cruiser. Loud rock music could be heard through The Trunk Lid's thick concrete walls. They readied their gear and strapped on their helmets. Otis handed an extra pair of handcuffs and plastic flex-ties to each officer.

"We go in two abreast," Otis said. "Roger and me first. We stay together at all times, no matter what. Arrest anyone who gives us trouble or won't produce ID or is using dope. When we check the men's room, two go in, two on guard outside the door."

Otis keyed the mic of his portable radio. "Three Zero Nine to Four-Twenty."

"Go ahead," Sergeant Breen answered.

"We're going in."

"Received."

Cigarette and marijuana smoke permeated the air. Dim lights and the sultry music of Santana's "Black Magic Woman" resonated off the walls. The bouncer at the door had burly tattooed arms, Bandido colors on the back of his denim vest, a red bandana on his forehead, greasy jeans, heavy black Wellington boots. He glared and clenched his meaty fists when the four-man team strode in, helmeted, two abreast.

The crowd near the door was taken aback. Nervous mutterings could be heard along with four-letter expletives, but no one challenged them. The crowd parted like water as the four moved deeper into the cavern as a unit, where more than a dozen couples were dancing.

Otis saw Hitchcock suddenly stop and stare at the dance floor. He understood why when he looked at the crowd. *She* was there. Hitchcock's old flame, Ruby. Blonde, sensual, voluptuous. Most women needed plastic surgery to be half as attractive.

Men stood in a circle watching her. She put on a show for them, flaunting her figure. Her dance partner, a thin, under-muscled, ratty-looking youth with a peace symbol on his shirt. Hitchcock stood, mesmerized, and the lyrics of the Santana song fit the moment.

He flashed back to a golden time of innocence, before he knew Regret, and war, to a wild love affair with a golden-haired girl, older than himself, to wedding plans that never happened. But Ruby didn't see him. He turned at a nudge on his elbow, the "we're here on business" message in Otis's eyes brought Hitchcock back to reality and duty. For a moment Ruby had him mesmerized. Only through his military discipline could he step away from her.

They moved deeper into the crowd, bold but not pushy, purposeful but not swaggering. The unspoken message was *"We're here on business and we're in charge,"* and the crowd knew it.

Hitchcock spotted a long-haired, bearded male standing outside the men's room, as if guarding it, nervously puffing on a cigarette as he watched the officers. Hitchcock nudged Otis. "Restroom!" he exclaimed.

The lookout rushed into the room when he saw officers moving fast in his direction. Hitchcock and Otis charged through the door, into a cloud of marijuana smoke, knocking the "guard" into the wall where three men stood, two of them simultaneously flushing toilets.

"Hands on the wall, spread your feet," Otis commanded as he and Hitchcock spun them to face the wall. He stood guard while Hitchcock searched them. On two men, he found marijuana pipes and plastic baggies containing what surely was marijuana.

The third man had about a half ounce of white powder in a clear plastic baggie in his shirt pocket. Seizing the baggie, Hitchcock held it up to the man's face. "What's this? Heroin?"

"It's just a little coke, man. I don't do heroin."

"You're all under arrest for possession of controlled substance." Hitchcock recited their Miranda warning rights as Otis handcuffed them. They marched their four prisoners out the door. The shocked crowd nervously made way for them without a peep of challenge.

Sherman motioned for Otis to wait when he spotted a kid he knew from a recent shoplifting arrest to be a juvenile. The kid held a beer as he sat at a table with two girls and another male. Four Olympia beers were on the table.

"You're under arrest, Scott, minor in possession. Let's go," Sherman said. The kid shook his head and cursed under his breath as he got up from the table. Sherman cuffed him and handed him to Walker. He looked at the other three. They also looked too young to be there. "Let's see your IDs. Now," Sherman commanded. Only the other male was twenty-one. The two girls were underage. Borrowing handcuffs from Otis, Sherman arrested both girls.

The officers strode to the front door, seven handcuffed prisoners in tow. Unlike the previous night, the mutterings of protest coming from the crowd were soft-spoken and timid. The bouncer blocked the door as the team approached, glowering and clenching his fists.

"Make way or you'll be going with us," Walker stated matter-of-factly.

The bouncer crossed his arms in defiant refusal. He

was taller and heavier than Walker, but Walker brushed him aside with the edge of his forearm as easily as if he were a manikin.

"Do stick around. I won't be long," Walker promised as he held the door open for the team and their prisoners.

Otis radioed for patrol cars to transport prisoners to the station. Walker went back inside. He found the bouncer bragging to customers how he could have taken any of the officers in a fight.

"You're under arrest for obstructing a public officer," Walker told him. "You can come peaceably or the hard way. Choose the hard way and resisting arrest will be an added charge. Pick one."

Walker read in the bouncer's eyes that he would throw a punch with his right. He reached for the bouncer's arm with his left, and the punch came. Walker caught the fist in midair in his huge right hand and squeezed. The bouncer tried to jerk his hand back, but Walker's grip was too strong. He tried to throw a punch with his free hand but stopped when pain shot through his arm as Walker kept crushing his right fist. His knees buckled as Walker kept squeezing. A crackling sound like Rice Krispies in a bowl was heard as the cartilage between his knuckles broke.

The hushed crowd stayed back as Walker kept squeezing and the biker collapsed, crying and begging to be let go. Walker clapped the cuffs on him, and half-dragged him through the doors as a hushed crowd watched.

When Walker came out with a prisoner, Otis went in, citation book in hand. "Let's see your ID. Now," he commanded the bartender.

"What for?"

"For serving alcohol to minors. Refuse once, even hesitate, and I'll take you to jail and close this place down and the state liquor board will hear about it."

Otis cited him and returned to his men and the prisoners outside.

IT TOOK AN hour to book every prisoner, write reports and fill out lab request forms for drug testing. Hitchcock turned to Otis as they finished. "My gut instinct tells me we should go back to The Lid," he said.

Otis nodded. "Me too. You drive."

As they left the station, Otis asked, "was that who I think it was on the dance floor tonight?"

Hitchcock swallowed hard. Both hands on the wheel. He hesitated, then answered "Yep."

"Must've been hard to see her in a dump like that. Dancing with a piece of walking roadkill. Ruby's so different I didn't recognize her at first."

Hitchcock sighed and kept his eyes on the road. "It's like a supernatural wind blew through the country while we were away. The war changed us, changed everything; it couldn't be otherwise in these times. For better or worse, Ruby and I've taken different paths. We're different people now. What we had is gone."

Otis nodded, "Still, I could see it bothered you to see her like that."

"It bothered me," he acknowledged at last, keeping his eyes on the road.

Otis looked out the window at the passing scenery. It had been a busy night. "These times have reshaped us all, kid," he said, "and there's more to come."

It was 1:14 a.m. when they cruised past The Trunk Lid on the four-lane Bel-Red Road. Only a few cars were still there. Hitchcock continued up the road until The Trunk Lid was out of sight in his rearview mirror, then hung a left at the next side street and doubled back. He approached slowly on a narrow two-lane street that ran parallel to the Bel-Red, passing small closed industrial shops.

He killed the headlights when he entered the upper parking lot of a boat repair shop where they could look down into The Trunk Lid parking lot.

They hid their cruiser among boats and boat trailers, facing the Trunk Lid. In silence they scanned the parked cars with binoculars. Nothing. They waited. Then two young men came out of the bar and got into a car which was parked facing the front of the building. Seconds later a flame inside the car flared briefly, then flickered out, its orange glow momentarily illuminating the two men in the front seat.

"Look at that! They're shooting up, Joel!"

"Let's sneak on down there and bust 'em."

They quietly eased out of their patrol car, heavy-duty Kel-Lite flashlights in hand, bending low as they crept among boats and trailers, down a rocky embankment to the lower lot, and slunk, bent over, among other parked cars until they reached their target.

"Take the driver's side, I'll take the passenger," Otis whispered. "We'll put our lights on 'em at the same time."

Hitchcock moved along in a crouch until he reached the rear edge of the driver's door. He and Otis stood up and shone their flashlights into the car at the same time. The driver had his left arm bared and extended, palm up, surgical tubing tied above the elbow, his right hand in the process of inserting a syringe into his left arm at the elbow.

"Police! You're under arrest!" Hitchcock shouted as he ripped open the door and jerked the needle out of the shocked suspect's arm.

Otis opened the passenger door at the same instant. An acrid smell hit him as he shined his flashlight in the other man's eyes, blinding him as he shouted, "You're under arrest. Hands behind your head!" Hitchcock pushed the lighter, needle, spoon, and a plastic baggie of white powder from the driver's lap to the floor and pulled him out of the car by the front of his shirt.

They handcuffed and searched both suspects. The

one Hitchcock arrested began fidgeting and rolling his head side to side, shifting his weight from one foot to the other, straining against the cuffs.

"Awww, officerrrr!" he whined. "You don't know what you've duuhhn! I need my fiiix! Let me go, pleeease! I'm gonna *die* if you don't! C'mon, I'll do anything, tell you anything you want to know if you let me go."

"Shut up, Howie!" the other man snarled.

A small crowd leaving the bar gathered around. Keeping one hand on his prisoner, Otis faced the crowd. "Keep moving. Nothing here concerns any of you."

Hitchcock left and came back with the black-and-white. The crowd had dispersed except for two shaggy-haired young men, hands in their pockets, who were arguing with Otis as he held on to both prisoners. Hitchcock got out of the cruiser and stood between them and Otis. "These men are our prisoners and you are interfering," Hitchcock said. "Stand back. Now."

"Hey, man, be cool. We just wanna know why–"

Hitchcock stepped right into his face. "Shut–up," he demanded. "Stand back or I arrest you both for interfering with a public officer. Move it!"

With their hands in their pockets in an "aw shucks" manner, they glanced at each other, shrugged, turned and shuffled away without a word, meek as mice.

Howie descended into uncontrollable agitation, moaning and crying, itching, hopping from one foot to the other, muttering to himself, making it harder for Otis to hold him and the other prisoner. His forehead glistened with sweat; his nose dripped, he trembled and babbled incoherently.

Otis checked his pulse. It was racing and his pupils were pinpoints, even in the low light. He removed the cuffs from behind and cuffed Howie's hands in front.

"Here, Howie," Otis led him to the back door of the cruiser. "Sit on the back seat of our car, lay down if you want, while we get a ride to take you to the hospital. You're gonna be all right."

Hitchcock clicked handcuffs on the other suspect and put on plastic gloves to gather the drugs and paraphernalia he and Otis had seized.

Otis eased Howie into the back seat, laid him down and grabbed the radio mic. "Radio, send another unit Code Two to the Trunk Lid parking lot. We have a male adult in heroin withdrawal who needs prompt medical attention at the ER. We have another in custody for felony drug possession."

Sergeant Breen was on the road when he heard Otis's transmission. He shook his head with pleasure and laughed out loud. "Damn if they didn't go right back out and pop that sewer again when it was least expected! Delstra's gonna love it when he reads this!"

A FEW MINUTES past 4:00 a.m., Walker entered the squad room where Hitchcock and Otis were finishing their reports, having logged in evidence and booked their prisoner for the morning shift to take to the county jail. "The boys are gettin' together at my place for a few. Join us," Walker said.

Hitchcock looked at Otis, who replied, "We'll be there."

"What happened to Forbes tonight?" Hitchcock asked Walker.

Walker shrugged. "Why?"

"Didn't hear him on the air all night," Hitchcock said. "Didn't hear him call in service, and we still were on the air and heard everybody signed off but him. So where is he?"

"Come to think of it, I saw Mark head toward the west side in his cruiser at the start of the shift, but I never heard him on the air." Walker said.

"Could he be taking his mistakes that hard?" Otis asked.

"Let's ask Breen," Hitchcock said.

Walker shook his head. "Jack already went home. I invited Mark to join us. Let's see if he shows up."

CHAPTER EIGHT
The After-Hours Fellowship

HITCHCOCK LED OTIS the seven blocks from the station to his former apartment, anxious to see what Walker had done with it.

Except for Forbes, the rest of the squad was there, cheerful, lounging, drinks in hand, civilian jackets over their uniforms. Hitchcock's eyes roved around the living room and kitchen, delighting in Walker's décor.

Unfinished two-by-six planks on concrete blocks covered an entire wall, floor to ceiling. Over fifty empty brown stubby Olympia and Rainier beer bottles were on the planks, like trophies. Thumb-tacked to another wall were black-and-white posters of Jack Webb as Sergeant Joe Friday on the TV show *Dragnet*, and Marilyn Monroe over a vent in a sidewalk, clutching her skirt as the draft of air blew it up to her waist. Posters of Billy the Kid and Sheriff Pat Garrett with their six-guns adorned the kitchen wall.

In the living room, a lived-in, slept-on brown corduroy couch, four chocolate brown beanbag chairs, and a hand painted "pet rock" on the dilapidated wood coffee table. Weights, including dumbbells, were stacked in the dining area.

"Interesting knick-knacks, do-dads and family photos you got here, Ira," Hitchcock said, tongue-in-cheek. "They give your place a real warm fuzzy feel. Cop-style ambience. Didn't know you had it in you. Did that pet rock come from a frizzy-haired hippie chick upstairs, goes by Willow, by any chance?"

Walker's eyebrows furrowed. "Yeah. You know her?"

"She gave me a pet rock, too."

"Yeah?... And?"

Hitchcock shook his head. "Nothing else. Met her once. A nice kid. Funky, but nice. For a hippie, she sure likes cops. But be careful. She's into snakes too, and pot, I assume."

"Her snake is gone or I wouldn't be around. In my current position I can't be as choosy as you."

Walker gestured to the array of bottles on the kitchen counter. "Help yourselves. I got Rainier and Oly, vodka, bourbon and scotch, lime pop and ice, even a few clean glasses."

Hitchcock glanced around the room as he sat down with two fingers of Wild Turkey on ice. "Everybody's here 'cept Forbes. Where's Mark?"

"Pouting and feeling sorry for himself," snorted LaPerle with a shake of his head. "Feels he's been shelved after the trouble he got himself into at the Trunk Lid."

Otis settled into a beanbag chair, lit a cigar and took a sip of whiskey. "Mark's trying to prove himself to us," he said. "He's struggling with the fact that he doesn't know how to fight. What led to his need to prove himself at The Lid was losing the first fight of his life at the Village Inn. He can't get over it."

Allard chugged half of his fourth bottle of Oly and let out a long belch before chiming in. "Whaddya' mean he can't fight? Mark's real skookum, seen the size of his arms? Works out all the time."

"Lifting weights in front of a mirror is no substitute for skill, training and experience," Otis said.

Hitchcock, feeling the warmth of whiskey, waxed eloquent. "Mark's self-conscious, he doesn't have enough experience to know that some you win, some you lose. Wooten got knocked out of the same fight right off, just like Mark did, but Lee knows from experience that you can't win 'em all. When you lose, you use the loss as a lesson for the next time."

"Yup, that's right, Roger," Wooten agreed, smiling groggily. "Nobody likes losing. Fact is, there's always somebody better or luckier than you. It ain't the end of the world."

Sherman, being the first to begin imbibing, was

oiled up good and proper. "Mark's a good guy," he said, "but he needs to leave that frou-frou gym, and learn to box or go in the Army for a while. Then come back."

"He can't," Otis interjected. "Mark's got a wife and two kids. They're the reason he stayed home when we went away. If he wasn't past his probation, the Brass would fire him. He's got Civil Service protection now, so the Department has to have just cause to let him go. The Brass and the third-floor crowd are watching him and they won't be happy when they learn of the stupid risks he took at the Trunk Lid. His lack of judgment really is a liability to the City."

"Mark handled himself well at a juvenile party we were called to night before last," LaPerle said. "Most of the teeny-boppers were zonked out on dope, laying on furniture, or the floor or wherever. Mark caught and arrested the adult who hosted the party to have his pick of doped-up underage girls. Caught him in the act with an underage girl in one of the bedrooms."

Hitchcock shook his head. "One good felony arrest won't get Mark off the hotseat. We're worried and the Brass is rightfully worried. His need to prove himself could get all of us in a lawsuit, which is why they might use this latest thing to let him go."

"I'll be surprised if they don't," Otis said.

"The Brass is responsible for weighing the risks of keeping officers like Mark on," Hitchcock continued. "He'll lose his job if he keeps on this way. Like Joel said, he's got a wife and two little kids. He needs our help, or he won't make it. I propose we all agree to keep an eye on him and help him, so he doesn't overreact and get himself killed or fired."

"If Mark doesn't get a reset we'll lose him," Otis remarked.

"I agree. Let's all drink to Forbes getting a reset!" Sherman cheered, hoisting his glass in the air.

"Yeah, a toast. To keepin' Forbes among us!" slurred Allard as he tried to stand and fell back into his chair, almost dropping his sixth or seventh beer.

"And I propose we all help Allard by not standing up as we drink to Forbes," LaPerle said, to everyone's cheers.

"It's this beanbag chair, not me, Frenchie," Allard said sheepishly.

"Yeah, right!" LaPerle said in his usual hearty way when he drank. "We're makin' a pact to help our buddy Forbes, and seal it with a toast!" LaPerle announced cheerily. He held his glass in the air with all the others and said, "Here's to our brother Mark Forbes! We all swear to help him stay among us. May he have the presence of mind to listen to us." The sound of glass clinking against glass went around the room.

Wooten changed the subject. "What's with the generation right behind us?" he asked. "When we were their age, we drank, we partied wild, laughed and had fun. None of us even thought about dope. When these kids get together, it's pills or shots of whatever, and they're on their way out. They get zonked out like…" Wooten laid back, spreading his feet and arms out and his head back.

"The latest thing is 'blotter acid,'" Walker said. "Friday night I got a call to a house where the son, seventeen, was scaring the crap out of his parents and his sister. He was on LSD. I arrested him and, in his pants pocket, I found three squares of paper that had single dots on them. Took them with me when I took him to Harborview, where the doc told me the dots are the newest form of LSD. Almost impossible to detect. Put the paper in the mouth, the acid dissolves. Apparently, it was this kid's third time on acid and he took two that night. Doc said he'll probably have brain damage."

"The doc is right," Hitchcock said. "LSD causes permanent brain damage. In the middle of the brain is the reticular activating system. RAS for short. Its function is overall awareness and mental arousal, including sleep levels. The RAS is governed by a fluid the brain makes called serotonin."

Hitchcock paused when he noticed his mates looking at each other with raised eyebrows. "Hey – are you guys okay with my explaining this? We're here to relax before going home, so tell me if I oughta shut up, and I will."

"You're fine, keep going," Sherman encouraged as he poured himself another drink.

"What LSD does is mimic serotonin," Hitchcock continued. "When LSD is present, the brain synapses become crowded with too much serotonin-like substance, allowing for impulses to be created and go to the higher levels of the brain, the cerebral cortex, so the person sees things that aren't really there. Hallucinations, which the brain interprets as real. People keep doing it for the pleasant effects it can produce, but long-term, permanent brain damage is very likely. Already there are cases of people who took LSD only once who will probably have flashbacks for the rest of their lives when they see a certain color or hear a certain sound."

LaPerle, six-sheets-to-the-wind by now, turned his bleary eyes to Hitchcock. "How do you know all this?" he asked woozily. "I know you wuz a medic in the Army, so izzat whut they taught'cha?"

"I can answer that," Walker interrupted, wearing a proud big brother grin. "Roger's girlfriend – or I should say *one* of his girlfriends – is a 'doctaahh' at the Overlake ER. A real MD. She makes boo-coo bucks, and she's crazy about Roger."

After the "ooohs," "ahhhs," and "attaboys" subsided, a grinning Hitchcock said, "Okay, boys, sure, I'm dating Rhonda Kringen. She's been educating me about the drugs we're seeing on the street, and I've been reading up on it."

LaPerle, always the comedian when he drank, couldn't stop snickering. "Rhonda's been 'educating' you; you say. Hah! I've been to the ER when she's there. She's a *stone fox* with a stethoscope! Easy on the eyes but hard on the heart. I got an idea, maybe she should put on a drug education class for us at the station, but on second thought, what if your wives found out? Me? I'm single."

Wooten leaned further back in his beanbag chair, his face slack with scotch, mischief in his grin. "Don't know how I fit in here, boys. You see, I'm not married, but my wife is!" Everyone laughed.

Explaining the effects of LSD downshifted Hitchcock's mood to morose thoughts of schoolmates and childhood friends either dead, dying or becoming brain damaged in the wake of the new drug culture. They were caught in a vacuum of values changing at warp speed. Life was becoming meaningless for them and society was becoming more polarized than ever. He perceived the current troubles as a bottomless pit. He shook his head and finished his drink. The others stopped talking as he stood and put on his jacket. "See you boys Monday night, I'm taking comp time tonight," he said on his way out.

HE FOUND JAMIE waiting faithfully in front of the carport, rain-soaked, wagging his tail joyfully when he rounded the last bend, of the driveway to the cabana.

"Hey, Jamie boy. Waitin' for me, eh?" he said, rough-rubbing his hands over Jamie's head and neck, at which the dog happily leaned into his master's leg. "I'll rustle up some grub, then I gotta catch a few winks."

The phone rang as he set a metal bowl full of hamburger and dried kibble in front of Jamie.

"Officer Hitchcock?" a female voice inquired.

"Yes. Who is this?"

"Patty, from Records. A woman came here about an hour ago. Asked us to give you a message to call her. She left her number. Said her name is Ruby, and that you know her."

Hitchcock's pause was long. There was only the sound of Jamie's nose in his stainless-steel bowl, licking up the last chunk of hamburger.

"Officer Hitchcock, are you still there?"

"Yes, sorry. I'm here. She came to the station?"

"She came to the public window," Patty replied. "Who is she, may I ask?"

"What did she look like?"

Patty hesitated. "She reminded me of Dolly Parton."

He felt a knot in his stomach. *I'll never get to sleep now.* "Give me the number and also leave it in my inbox."

CHAPTER NINE
Meeting the Chattertons

THE KNOT IN his stomach robbed him of the sleep he needed. The clock on his nightstand read 10:00 a.m. Late. The dramatic arrests of the night before weren't on his mind—it was Ruby. He laid on his bed, dressed in sweats and socks, staring at the ceiling, listening to the rain on the roof, thinking, *she came to the station to leave a message for me. Why didn't she call instead?*

She wanted to see him. *Why?* The way he saw her at the Trunk Lid troubled him. She had changed. He didn't know how he felt about seeing her again. He thought he was over the loss of her, but now, as before, Ruby dominated his mind.

He set his alarm for 6:00 p.m. "Dinner at Mom's at seven," he reminded himself as he stretched out, staring at the ceiling.

As his body relaxed, and consciousness began slipping away, he returned to a pivotal moment in his life, an earth-moving first kiss, another lifetime ago, in a wooded glen by a babbling brook. The summer sun gleamed on the golden-haired girl of rare beauty from the Deep South, smiling, whispering, joyously pressing herself hungrily into his embrace. They were new to each other by merely hours, yet they were already as one.

Ruby began fading. As she became more transparent, he clung to her more tightly to keep her in his arms, where she belonged. He tried to tell her not to go, but the words wouldn't come. He tightened his arms around her, but in vain. Her loving green-blue eyes remained locked on his as she slowly vanished.

Sleep came to him then, dead and dreamless.

HE AWAKENED A few minutes before 6:00 p.m., refreshed and looking forward to seeing his family. He fed Jamie before he showered, dressed in gray gabardine wool slacks, starched pale blue pinstripe dress shirt, navy blue sport coat, black loafers, a splash of English Leather cologne. He cast a long look of consideration at Jamie, who had been wagging his tail as he watched his master's unusual preparations.

"Know what? You can come with me tonight, but you'll have to stay in our car. How's that suit you?" As if he understood every word, Jamie woofed and moved to the sliding glass door.

Before he left, Hitchcock strode back to his bedside nightstand and touched his late father's photograph. "Gonna see Mom, Jean and Joan and your grandchild, now, Dad. Thanksgiving dinner won't be the same without you," he said wistfully.

Jamie jumped into the passenger seat the second he opened the driver door. He fired up his gold '69 El Camino rumbled down the narrow eight-hundred-yard gravel road to the paved street. No traffic on Wilburton Hill at the moment. He rolled down SE 5th Street, which angled down to a stop sign at 116th Avenue, a four-lane road. The three-story Bellevue City Hall was on the other side of 116th. Traffic was light on a Sunday evening and the rain had stopped, leaving the streets dry. Hitchcock turned right, traveled two blocks and turned left at the signal at Main Street, taking the overpass over the 405 freeway.

Jamie sat upright on the passenger seat, staring out the windshield, turning his head at every pedestrian they passed on the sidewalk. Hitchcock tuned his AM radio to KAYO, the country music station. *The Bellevue Florist on Old Main Street is always closed on Sundays*, he thought as he entered the parking lot of the Mayfair store on 108th Avenue and Main that used to be the PX store.

He remembered his other uniform was still at the

Norge Dry Cleaners next to the Mayfair store, waiting to be picked up. He bought a colorful bouquet of flowers at Mayfair and headed north along four-lane 104th Avenue, the main drag through the almost empty downtown core.

Passing the main entrance to Bellevue Square on the left, and The Barb restaurant on the right brought back memories of dates with Ruby. Dinner at The Barb, where she always ordered prime rib, and movies at the John Danz or the Bel-Vue theaters. Boyhood memories returned when his eyes lingered on Sturtevant's Sporting Goods, Larkin's Five and Dime, and Harry's of San Francisco, a popular delicatessen, also on the right.

Hitchcock pondered the growth that had happened since he was a boy. The Puget Power building, Bellevue's tallest at four stories, still seemed like a skyscraper compared to the rest of the downtown. *But probably not for long*, he thought.

Even with the recent changes, original Bellevue still had a quaintness about it which he realized couldn't last, considering what he was seeing on its streets at night. Especially Eastgate. Part of Bellevue, but the freeway and its straight-shot proximity to Seattle separated it from the rest of the city, made it a natural thoroughfare for drugs and crime of all kinds that was spreading. The thought of it grieved him.

Seeing the Village Inn and the Marvel Morgan store on the corner as he waited at the signal at NE 8th Street, he smirked as he remembered the fight when he and Otis subdued Beecham and McMinn in a parking lot brawl two months ago.

Heading west on NE 8th Street, in four blocks he passed from the commercial district into residential zones; high-end homes in the Vue Crest neighborhood on the right, older homes on narrower streets and smaller lots were on the left.

He cruised downhill on NE 8th into the town limits of Medina, a wealthy suburb of Bellevue, where the streets seemed broader, the homes more palatial, on larger, well-groomed lots, the cars more expensive and of foreign make.

Childhood memories came back as he passed St. Thomas Episcopal, where his family attended until his father underwent a conversion or revival of sorts through Father Dennis Bennett, the pastor at St. Luke's Episcopal in Seattle. He remembered how the conversion changed his father's rather stoic disposition to one of lively passion that he liked, but never quite understood.

A few blocks past the church, Hitchcock arrived on time at his mother's home, a tidy, polished chocolate brown brick rambler in Medina, an upscale suburb of Bellevue which she bought after his dad's passing.

His sister Joan and her husband Darren's metallic blue Oldsmobile station wagon and the aqua Chevy Malibu belonging to his sister Jean, Joan's twin, were parked in the driveway, but he'd never seem the stately white Bentley sedan with New York plates before. He walked up to the front door, fresh flowers in hand, and rang the bell.

His sister Jean opened the door, holding her arms wide open. "Happy Thanksgiving, brother of mine, you stranger you!" she exclaimed and pulled him into a warm hug. Slipping her arm into his, as he neared the kitchen, he closed his eyes and inhaled. The aroma of roast turkey and side dishes simmering on the stove reminded him that he had been home from the war barely more than a year. He had missed Thanksgiving dinner with his family last year because of shift schedule. Now that he thought of it, he hadn't sat down to a home-cooked dinner with his family in over four years.

Slipping her arm into his, Jean walked him into the kitchen. "Hey everybody! Guess who's finally come around!"

Joan, Jean's identical twin, holding her infant son in her arms and her tummy swollen with another baby, smiled as she gave him a hearty one-arm hug. "Happy Thanksgiving, Roger, so good to see you. I'm glad Darren met you at the door. He's been looking forward to spending some time with you."

Hitchcock turned to his brother-in-law. "I see you're taking good care of my sister and increasing the family ranks, Darren. Now we've got to find somebody like you for Jean."

Jean laughed. "Hey now! Not so fast you two!"

"Yeah? Well, then, why isn't your beau, Matt, here?" Darren asked.

"You know the reason, Darren," Jean said. "He wouldn't come because he's afraid of Roger."

"I know what Matt told Jean, exactly," Darren proclaimed, his eyes twinkling mischief.

"What did he say, Darren?" Hitchcock asked, surprised.

"At the last minute, Matt called Jean and told her. "As the head eunuch said, 'I cannot come! I repeat, I cannot come!"

Amid the gales of laughter, Jean, herself laughing gently swatted Darren, and her brother for laughing.

"And I can see why!" Darren chuckled. "Seriously, Jean, he *ought* to be scared witless of Roger, and Roger should be screening your dates!"

"I'd wind up a spinster if he did," Jean said, eyes beaming lovingly at her brother.

Myrna left the stove for a moment to give her son a warm hug. "I'm so glad you came, Roger. Happy Thanksgiving. Say," she said, brushing his jacket with her hand, "you've got dog hair all over you!"

"You know what they say, Mom," he said, chuckling. "If you don't have dog hair on your clothes, you aren't properly dressed."

"My son, the comedian," Myrna replied cheerfully."

Let me introduce you to our guests." She led him into the living room. "Please meet Heath Chatterton and his family. Heath, this is my only son, Roger."

A bespectacled, slender man of medium height in his fifties with wavy, slicked-down, graying brown hair parted on the side, a dark mustache, bushy eyebrows, impeccably over-dressed in pleated brown plaid slacks, brown leather suspenders, white dress shirt with gold cuff links and a red bow tie, extended his delicate white hand. It felt cold and limp as a dead fish. He so reminded Hitchcock of the old-time cigar-smoking comedian Groucho Marx that he struggled to keep from laughing.

"I am pleased to finally meet you, Roger," Chatterton said, his New England accent as cold and brittle as his blue eyes. "I have heard so much about you from your mother, and I read in the papers about you too," he said with a tone of Eastern condescension. "I would like you to meet my wife, Ethel, and my daughter, Emily."

The sight of a matronly twenty-year-old, assembled as if from whatever spare body parts happened to be on hand, shocked him. Emily Chatterton was tall, flat bosomed with stout hips and legs, thin shoulders, long arms and long narrow flat feet that reminded Hitchcock of canoes. Dressed in a knee-length pink skirt and a long-sleeved, white silk blouse, she had short, mouse brown hair and wore thick glasses. She looked unreal, like a country schoolmarm in a stage play. She blushed behind her glasses. Hitchcock smiled politely as he shook her limp, sweaty hand, wondering what his mother could be thinking if she thought this is the girl for him.

"So nice to meet you, Roger," Emily said in a lesser trace of New England accent than her father.

"Ethel, this is Myrna's son, Roger," Chatterton said in a snide tone.

Hitchcock turned his attention to the other woman. Ethel Chatterton was the obvious origin of her daughter's physical shortcomings. Heavy-hipped, same horn-rimmed glasses, and short, curly salt-and-pepper hair. She wore a dark gray tweed dress suit and black, patent leather high-heeled shoes. "Hello, Roger. Your mother speaks of you often," she said, her face void of expression, her manner aloof and guarded, her words crisply accented with short, curled vowels like her husband's.

"Take your seats, everyone!" Myrna ordered. "Dinner is ready! Please sit where your name plate is. Jean, help me set the food out on the table, dear."

Hitchcock stepped into the dining room. The table was set. The family's fine white china, sterling silver flatware, "H" engraved on the handle of every piece, softly glowing candles, white tablecloth and linen napkins. He took in bowls of dressing, cranberry sauce, gravy and mashed potatoes, but his mouth salivated for his favorite, the huge golden-brown turkey on a holiday platter, partially sliced, its aroma filling the room. He could hardly wait.

He located his nameplate at the head of the table, opposite his mother. To his left, appropriately, he would soon realize, the nameplate read Heath. He inwardly shook his head and thought, *Mom, Mom, oh Mom, what are you thinking?* when he saw the nameplate on his right read Emily.

Being a gentleman, Hitchcock seated Emily before he took his seat. "Thank you," she murmured, blushing. Emily's eyes were looking down, but the eyes of others at the table were on him. He felt a twinge of irritation at his mother for setting him up on his first holiday dinner at home in years.

"Myrna, if it's all right, I would say the blessing for us all," Heath Chatterton offered.

"Please do, Heath."

Hitchcock noticed Heath glance at him as he cleared his throat. "Lord, we thank thee for this thy bounty, and forgive us all for the wrongs we do, especially this immoral war we are in. Amen"

An uneasy silence cloaked the table. Myrna fidgeted in her chair. Jean, Joan and Darren looked uneasily at Hitchcock, who ignored the bait. "Pass the turkey and gravy, Darren, I haven't eaten like this in a long time," he said.

Heath Chatterton wasted no time. "So, Roger, we

are close friends with someone at your department. He's a rising star there, soon to be chief. I'll bet you didn't know that."

"No," Hitchcock said, as he put a large slice of turkey on his plate, drenched it with gravy and took his first bite. "I didn't know that. Who would that be?"

A look of shock came over Chatterton's face. "Why, the man who runs the whole show there, of course. Rowland Bostwick. *Lieutenant* Bostwick, to *you*, of course. Being just a patrolman, you certainly wouldn't be aware, of course, how could you, that your leader's family is from The Hamptons, as we are. His family came over from England before the War of Independence, as ours did."

"Oh? Which side were they on–your relatives, I mean," Hitchcock asked.

Chatterton smirked as he replied, "We supported the British, of course."

"Why didn't they go to Canada, then?"

"Why should they? Others had paid the price, so they stayed."

Hitchcock stared in shocked disbelief at Chatterton. *Bostwick may be an unwitting tool of a few clever schemers upstairs, but he sure has this guy snowed*, he mused.

"But back to Rowlie. That's *Lieutenant* Bostwick, to *you*," Chatterton continued. "He's been cleaning up the drugs and violent crime in Bellevue, making arrests and directing the men on how they should do their duty, and they all look up to him. He does this behind the scenes as much as possible, to protect the current chief."

"Protect the current chief from what?" Hitchcock asked, incredulous.

"Why, from his political enemies, of course, so he can retire and hand his badge to Rowlie," Chatterton said, dismayed by Hitchcock's question. "Because he's a family friend, I get to hear all about everything. Confidentially, of course. I would *never* betray any secrets. I probably know more about your Depart-ment than you do," Chatterton said with a vapid, smug grin.

Hitchcock choked on his food trying to stifle an outburst of laughter. He covered his mouth with his linen napkin. Myrna leaned across the table in concern. "Quick, Darren! Slap him on the back. Are you all right, Roger?"

Clearing his throat as Darren thumped on his back, Hitchcock turned away to cough and get the smile off his face. *Is this guy a comedian?* he wondered. *If so, he's good.* "I'm fine, Mom. Thanks, Darren."

Regaining his composure, Hitchcock asked Chatterton, "So Bostwick tells you these things, does he?"

"Yes, and again, he's *Lieutenant* Bostwick to *you*," Chatterton condescended, "but he's *Rowlie* to *us*. He's one of *us*. Indeed, a *fine* man. He'll be the next chief, right after Sean Carter retires. Says he's got it all locked up, thanks mostly to the city manager, whose wife is *also* from The Hamptons. Rowlie meets with the city manager quite a bit these days. Says he'll make a lot of changes in the Department, clean it up right away."

Hitchcock struggled to conceal the shock and amusement coursing through his mind. "He does, does he? What 'cleaning up' would Bostwick do? Did he tell you?"

"Yes, of course, as always," Chatterton chortled, his face beaming with self-importance. "Now, no offense, Roger, but Rowlie thinks the department shouldn't hire war veterans. Military people are too dangerous. And I am not the only one in the city who agrees with him. Men who have been in combat are damaged goods, so to speak. A pity, certainly, but any of you are liable to go on a rampage at any time. We should keep veterans at a safe distance from the rest of us."

A shocked silence fell upon everyone at the table. Joan gasped. "How could you say such a thing, Heath?" she asked. "It's cruel, and traitorous." Others at the table muttered their agreement. Myrna fluffed her cloth napkin, red-faced, jaw muscles flexing as she grit her teeth.

Chatterton glanced at Joan, gave her a condescending smirk and said nothing.

"Really? Who should protect you, then, from enemies, foreign and domestic, Heath?" Hitchcock asked.

Chatterton ignored the question.

"What is your profession, Heath?" Hitchcock asked as he spooned gravy over his second helping of mashed potatoes.

Chatterton stopped, his fork in med-air, to look at Hitchcock. "My profession?"

"Yes, how do you make your living?"

"I would have thought you'd understand, Roger, that there is a class of people who are above work, as you understand it," Chatterton said as he helped himself to another slice of turkey. "But I see you don't, so I will relieve you of your ignorance."

"Oh, so you're retired, then?" Hitchcock pressed in.

"Have you ever heard of The Chatterton Foundation? Surely you have."

Hitchcock smiled. "Nope. Can't say as I have. I have a sneaking suspicion you're going to tell us, so go ahead."

"Our family's wealth. It goes back two hundred years. I manage it. I'm above work," Chatterton said, smiling smugly.

"What does the Foundation do, exactly?" Hitchcock asked.

"We fund certain political movements from proceeds earned by the Foundation's investments."

"Political movements?" Hitchcock echoed.

"One of our crown jewels was Cuba in '59," Chatterton said.

"But back to our good friend Rowlie Bostwick. He

says he'll flush out the war veterans on the Bellevue force," he continued, "and hire only non-military people so that all of us are safe. Officers will wear slacks, white shirts and neckties, with blue sport coats instead of those military-looking uniforms. He'll also disarm the officers. They will only carry non-lethal things like clubs and sprays. Guns will be held in the station, released only when there is an emergency. That's how the Brits operate, and it works well for them."

"Except this is America, not Britain."

"Ah, yes," Chatterton continued in a sing-song lilt as he sawed off another hunk of turkey for himself. "But by disarming the police first," he said, pointing one finger in the air in the manner of a brown-nosing kid in a fourth grade classroom, "we set a precedent of good will that will be returned. The basic good that is in every man will respond in kind, except for a few exceptions, and all this violence nonsense will drop sharply."

Hitchcock looked around the table. His family members, sullen, staring at their plates, not eating. Chatterton's wife and daughter were also mute, but eating as if nothing was happening. Finally, Darren, his brother-in-law, made eye contact with Hitchcock. After a few seconds Darren nodded his head at Chatterton, his eyes still on Hitchcock.

"Let me see if I understand what you are saying, Heath," Hitchcock said. "Let's say there's two stick-up men holding up a state liquor store at gunpoint and they begin shooting any clerk or customer who looks at them. The police go to the scene, see what is happening, and instead of going in to confront the criminals, they must leave the scene to get their guns from the station and then return. Meanwhile more victims are killed. Is that what you want for people?"

"Oh my," Chatterton's wife gasped. Emily appeared to be on the verge of tears.

"You didn't need to be so graphic, Roger," Chatterton mumbled defensively.

Hitchcock could hardly believe his ears. He considered explaining to Chatterton that no chief can arbitrarily fire officers, especially for being veterans. He wanted to explain that officers are protected from arbitrary firing by the Civil Service Commission, and that the rate of officers killed on duty is up sharply since the late '60s. He decided he could learn more by holding his silence and letting Chatterton talk. As he expected, Chatterton kept chattering as he ate.

"So, Roger, I read in the paper about your beating up that poor Indian fellow a few weeks ago, and a later article about your boxing career. How was it?"

"How was what?"

"Boxing."

"Great. I've learned a lot about life from boxing. My dad boxed semi-professionally before and after the war. He paid his way through medical school with the prize money he won. He taught me the basics, and then I trained weekly at the club in Seattle where he trained, and also at home with a coach almost every day after school. I boxed competitively for nine years."

Hitchcock glanced down the table at his mother. She was beaming at him with pride. "My son won several championships in Golden Gloves, and went to the sixty-four Olympics. For years he trained hard. His grades were all A's except for a few B's, and he graduated from high school as an honor student" she said.

"I see," Chatterton said, focused on his plate.

"As for 'beating up' the man in the Village Inn parking lot, as you put it, Heath," Hitchcock continued, purposely calling him by his first name, "I used only enough force to stop him. It happened as the paper said; he and his partner beat and kicked four people to the pavement. One was a woman and three were police officers. Beecham was beating and kicking an officer who was down when I arrived. He'd be dead or a vegetable if I hadn't intervened. Beecham tried to do the same to me, but I prevailed."

His sister Jean cut in. "I think what you and Joel did was heroic, Roger, you both prevented further injury and may have saved lives."

"Oh yes, Otis. The other officer," Chatterton said, his voice dripping disdain. "We mustn't leave *him* out of our discussion. Myrna tells me his family lived next door to you when you were growing up. He is a few years older than you and had an influence on your decision to become a police officer."

Hitchcock nodded. "Joel is the older brother I never had. He taught me to play baseball when we were kids."

But Chatterton was thinking ahead to the next button to push rather than listen. "You were in Vietnam. What do you think of the war?"

Myrna interjected: "Excuse me, Heath, but this is Thanksgiving. Shouldn't we change to more pleasant subjects?"

"It's all right, Mom, I'll answer Heath's question." Hitchcock set his fork down on the half-eaten plate of food. He wiped his mouth with the linen napkin and set it down, then turned his gaze on Chatterton.

"I agree with the war, Heath. I've been there twice, a year each time; volunteered both times. Been on the ground. I've seen what kind of people the communists are. They don't share our values or think the way we do. To them, the ends always justifies the means, so it isn't wrong for them to lie, steal or kill to achieve their goals. That's why they are cruel, and skilled at wearing their enemies down. Psychologically as well as militarily."

Hitchcock paused. Chatterton set his folded napkin alongside his plate and kept smoothing it with his hand. His wife and daughter both fidgeted in their seats, saying nothing. Darren broke the silence. "I'm proud of you for being there, Roger. Wish I could have been there with you."

Hitchcock paused. When Chatterton glanced at him,

he continued. "Communism's been spreading since the end of the war, Heath. It's better to fight it over there than here. The biggest threat to our winning in Vietnam is the biased news media and weak politicians, not the communist forces in Asia. We've won every time on the battlefield, but we're losing the war at home and that's what the communists are counting on."

"I agree with you, Roger," Darren said in support. "If not for meeting Joan, I'd still be in uniform."

"Whether you know it or not, Roger, the world is changing," Chatterton said. "The progression toward unionism in this country will lead to socialism and later to a modified form of communism. The gospel will be preached, but a *social* gospel, not the antiquated Christian kind, but one of equality and share-and-share-alike, enforced by a benevolent government, and a ruling class, supported by news media, print and broadcast. The wasteful wars of the past will have served our purpose and won't exist anymore. Poverty will be a thing of the past. There will be no borders, no nations. One world. It's the future."

"You obviously think so, but the numbers say you're wrong."

Chatterton's arrogant smile evaporated. In a voice of cold condescension, he said "I believe in the factuality of numbers, Roger. Proceed, please."

"It's simple math, Heath. Take the so-called antiwar movement. The estimated total of participants in the protests is in the thousands, wouldn't you say?"

"Most surely. Tens of thousands," Chatterton agreed.

"And our present military population, most of whom aren't there as a career, is just under four million," Hitchcock continued. "Those three-plus million volunteers and draftees are perpetually rotating through the ranks. They are constantly being replaced with new people on a monthly basis, nearly all of whom support the war, or they wouldn't be there. The protestors' numbers are miniscule compared to the numbers of my generation who serve voluntarily. The real reason the protestors seem so dominant is due to news media bias and sensationalism, and those who exploit the turmoil to meet a hidden agenda. Such as yours."

"Excellent point, Roger!" Joan said, clapping.

"Never thought of it that way, but that's right," Darren added.

Even Ethel Chatterton was nodding in silent agreement, looking down, lips pursed.

A scowl replaced Chatterton's smugness. His face blushed red with anger and embarrassment. He lapsed into a grim silence for long seconds, trying but unable to think of something to say to recover the upper hand.

Hitchcock waited for Chatterton to respond, hoping he would accept the truth.

"Okay, so it is, we're a minority. A noisy one,"

Chatterton finally conceded. "But there are many of us in positions of influence who want America to lose this war and are working toward that goal. Secretly, of course. It's time America got a comeuppance. We're working behind the scenes to shape public opinion in that direction, away from our past. What do you think of that?"

Hitchcock looked calmly at Chatterton. "Who is this 'we' you refer to?"

Chatterton looked away. "Certain wealthy people. People who envision a brighter future for humanity. Who have enough money and influence to control world events."

"They sound like old fashioned capitalists to me, Hitchcock remarked.

"Correct," Chatterton said. "So, what do you think of our plan?"

"It's not what I think. It's what it is. Those who scheme against the country in wartime are aiding the enemy. It's called *treason*, Heath."

Chatterton glanced at his wife, who remained silent, looking down, hands in her lap, food barely touched. He looked at Myrna, his hostess. To Hitchcock's appreciation, she was red with boiling anger. Chatterton looked at Emily. She too had been quiet throughout the meal, and barely ate. Tears of hurt and embarrassment filled her eyes. She had looked forward to meeting Hitchcock, but thanks to her father, the evening hadn't gone at all as she had hoped.

Hitchcock amiably visited with his family for the rest of the dinner. When Myrna and Jean brought coffee and pumpkin pie, Hitchcock engaged Emily and Ethel in casual conversation. He tried to include Heath, but he withdrew into the family room, alone and sullen. At the end of another hour, Hitchcock kissed his mother and his sisters goodbye, shook hands with Darren, and did his best to be cordial to the Chattertons.

As Hitchcock headed out the door, his brother-in-law followed him. "Your mom looks real upset with Heath, Roger, like she's about to explode. Can't remember ever seeing her so mad. I think I'll ask Chatterton as he leaves how he enjoyed his first and last dinner with the Hitchcock clan. Whaddya think?"

Hitchcock laughed as he opened the passenger door of his El Camino and Jamie bounded out. The dog sniffed Darren, who stood still, then found a bush on which to relieve himself. As Jamie explored Myrna's lawn and flowerbeds, Hitchcock playfully jabbed Darren in the gut. "Nah, let it go with Heath. I purposely gave him enough rope to hang himself with Mom, and he did. Besides, I needed a good chuckle, and Heath supplied that in spades. I hope he isn't as serious about communism and treason as he let on."

Darren stepped closer to Hitchcock. "Did you know Heath and his wife are registered communists, Roger?"

"No, but I figured that from the way he talked

tonight."

"Did you know Heath and his wife are both wealthy heirs, neither has ever worked, yet they control a multi-million-dollar foundation?"

Stunned, Hitchcock shook his head, hands in his pockets, waiting for what Darren would tell him next.

"Don't you wonder why moneyed big shots from New England have gathered way out here, in a backwater state like Washington, with no apparent purpose? This ambitious lieutenant on your department *just happens* to also be from the same part of New York as the Chattertons, *and* the city manager?"

Hitchcock could only stare at his brother-in-law. "How do you know all this Darren?"

"As you know, I was in Army Intelligence in Germany. I still have contacts. I'm not saying any more, so don't ask."

"What can I do about it? I'm just a rookie," Hitchcock said after a pause.

Darren stared at Hitchcock for long seconds. "Watch your back, Roger," he said as he turned to go.

Hitchcock stared after him. "I'll do that. See ya, Darren."

† † †

THE WEATHER TURNED cold and rainy as he drove back to his digs. A perfect night to build a fire, sit back with a hot drink and relax. He toweled off and fed Jamie, then reheated the morning's coffee. The fir logs crackled and poured forth dry heat.

He settled in his favorite chair and put his feet up by the fire, cup in hand. The rain pattered on the roof, and he smiled as he pondered his conversation with Heath Chatterton, whose strong communist sympathies came as a surprise to everyone at the table. Everyone, except Chatterton's wife and daughter. Before Darren told him what he knew of the Chattertons, he had wondered if Heath actively supported subversive groups.

Hitchcock laughed out loud when he thought of the lighter side of the evening, Chatterton said Bostwick was "cracking down on crime" and "leading the men," and his plans to "clean up" the Department.

His thoughts turned to Ruby. He tossed another log on the fire and added whiskey to his coffee. *I've come a long way since the 'Dear John' letter she sent me while I was ducking bullets in 'Nam. Ended everything between us, so why should I call her?* he thought. *Seeing her for those few seconds, proved I'm still not over losing her. Maybe I never will be.*

As the fire dimmed to embers, old romantic scenes of being with Ruby returned. He lingered with her in those scenes a long time. Eventually the fire ebbed and the cabana grew cold. He would see her tomorrow, but it would be different than seeing her in old memories, like an old family movie, images flickering on a screen. That was what he preferred, the way it was, before the war, the way it *should* have been. If only, if only...if, if, if.

He had to leave Ruby now. Cold reality called. Until next time, and she would always be there, waiting for him.

CHAPTER TEN
You Can't Unscramble Eggs

THE DEAFENING RACKET of monsoon-level rain pounding the roof, and Jamie's wet nose pressing against his face the next morning, ended Hitchcock's sleep. He glanced at his clock, surprised to see he had slept ten hours straight. He arose, rested and clear-headed. He let Jamie out, refilled his percolator, making coffee extra strong, hit the splash locker, toweled off, dressed, then poured and drank his coffee black. After a moment's hesitation, he dialed Ruby's number. A number he would always remember.

A voice he would recognize anywhere answered on the second ring.

"Hello?"

Feeling his pulse rising at the sound of her voice after so much time, he cleared his throat. "Good morning, Ruby, it's Roger. I got your message to call you."

"Hello, Roger. I'm glad you called," Ruby said. "I've never forgotten you. I think about you all the time, you know."

For a few seconds he couldn't speak. "Me too," he finally said, voice cracking.

"After I saw you in the bar Saturday night, I thought we could see each other and just talk a bit."

"Sure. When?"

"How about today? One o'clock? I'm off work so that would be good for me."

"Where?"

"Remember the Hotel Café in Redmond? It'll be quiet there after the lunch crowd leaves."

He agreed before he hung up and sat on the edge of his bed, fully dressed, listening to the heavy rain. Memories of her and simpler times came back as he stared at the black-and-white photograph on his nightstand of himself as a little boy with his father and Bill Chace on the opening day of the Pancake Corral. He held the photograph by its brass frame, and touched the image of his dad, wishing he could somehow go back in time to ask his father's advice. He needed it.

THE TORRENTIAL DOWNPOUR thundered on the roof of his El Camino loud enough to drown out his radio, making headlights necessary for the thirty-minute drive to Redmond. The heat of Jamie's wet body as he laid on the front seat steamed up the windshield.

He flipped the defrost switch to high and wiped down the inside of the windshield with the cuff of his shirt, the rear window and both door windows with the rag he kept under the seat so he could see his mirrors.

He cruised at low speed down the gravel road to the pavement. He had to wait almost a minute at the stop sign at the bottom of the hill before he could merge into traffic. His defrost fan kept the windshield clear but the door and back windows fogged up, making his mirrors useless.

Too risky to take the freeway to Redmond with fogged up windows like this, he thought. He drove past Overlake Hospital and turned right, emerging into medium traffic.

At the stoplight at the four lane Bellevue-Redmond Road, he wiped down his door and back windows with the same rag, and turned right at the signal. Traffic thinned out two miles later as the road curved left and sloped downhill until Lake Sammamish came into view. A mile and a half later, he turned right, crossing over the Sammamish Slough into the town of Redmond.

Time seemed to have stood still in Redmond, a sleepy, rural burg ten miles by rural road from and east of Bellevue. There was still the V&B grocery store, the only one in town, the Mond Theater, the only one in town, the golf course and the brick two-story Hotel Café, which never closed.

Entering the '50s vintage town, he knew by heart the

rest of the way to where Ruby's family lived. *I could drive there with my eyes shut even now,* he realized.

Work in the Seattle shipyards and certain circumstances at home brought the Cain family to Washington from Mississippi in the early '60s. The reason for such an unprecedented move was undisclosed, but rumors had it that it had something to do with Ruby's father, Virgil, and the Klan.

A close-knit family; the Cains lived in the Northwest in much the same manner as they did in the South, on wooded acreage about five miles east from town on Novelty Hill Road, with chickens, a large vegetable garden and fruit trees. Virgil drove a dark gray late '40s Dodge pickup with a rifle in a rack in the back window, kept a Bluetick tracking hound, and smoked a pipe. Ruby was the eldest of four kids and the most stunning.

The storm absorbed Hitchcock's anxiety as he drove to the meeting, but his heart lodged in his throat. He braced himself to hear things from Ruby he didn't want to hear, just as on Saturday at The Trunk Lid, he saw her in ways he wished he hadn't.

The décor in the Hotel Café resembled a Southern roadside diner. He picked a booth on the far side of the black and white checkerboard linoleum floor. The waitress brought two coffees.

He didn't have to wait long.

Ruby dominated the room the second she came through the door. She always did. Dressed casually in blue jeans and a tight black sweater which accentuated her dramatic figure, her honey-golden mane flowed over her shoulders and her blue-green eyes set in chiseled high cheekbone features swept the room until they locked on Hitchcock. Her smile was at once tense and open as she crossed the room. Old memories flooded over Hitchcock with her every step. He got to his feet as she approached and waited for her to sit down.

"Thanks for getting up. The men around here, if they can be called that, don't have manners anymore," she said as she slid into the seat.

Twinges of pain and longing filled Hitchcock when he heard her voice still had a trace of Southern accent. An awkward silence followed when her eyes met his. "So, I got to see you in your police uniform Saturday night," she said, breaking the stalemate. He had no words. He gazed at her as if seeing her for the first time.

"I didn't recognize you at first because of your helmet, but your build I would know anywhere," she said. "You looked strong and very handsome as always. And the way you guys took those idiots out of there was amazing. Did I see Joel, your former neighbor, with you?"

He nodded. "Joel convinced me to join Bellevue instead of Seattle when I came back."

"I thought I recognized him."

She tossed her hair back and Hitchcock inhaled,

catching her scent, more memories and yearning.

"You guys were clearly nobody to mess with. Four real men had all the blowhard 'little boys' so scared some probably peed their pants, especially when the bouncer everybody was so afraid of lost the use of his hand for a long, long time. That was something," Hitchcock watched the perfect, sensuous pair of lips as she chuckled.

"What's your connection to that place?" he asked, regret-ting the question as soon as he asked. He didn't really want to know.

"I date the two greedy slobs who own it. Both of them," she said casually, as if giving her opinion about the weather. "Those two really think they're cool. They hate cops and the law. They serve anybody and everybody who comes in, as you know, and they don't care what else goes on, no matter how illegal. The place is wide open, whatever you can think of goes on in there. They know your Department doesn't have undercover narcs. The owners and the customers say bad things about cops, Bellevue cops especially, but after last Saturday you might see a change in attitude."

As he listened to her, a lump formed in his throat. Her words about two men at one time in her life cut his heart to ribbons. Ruby, his first real love, was gone. *Who is this woman sitting in front of me, in Ruby's body?* He did not recognize this stranger who looked like the Ruby he knew long ago.

Ruby's eyes went over him appreciatively. "You're obviously taking good care of yourself," she said. "Women young and old must still fight over you, as they did when we were together. The one who lands you will be lucky."

He said nothing. Ruby sipped her coffee, looking at him. "So, will you return to boxing? You emerged as one of the top candidates in Seattle to turn pro after the Olympics, before your dad passed away."

He shook his head once. "Not enough time for it now. I train just enough to keep in shape."

"Let me guess. You're still doing a hundred pushups at a whack to warm up, like your dad taught you, right?"

He nodded with a grin. Suddenly her presence pleased him. Her eyes widened in wonderment. He boldly took in what he could of her, to which she smiled the way she used to. The lusty fire he once knew still lived, as embers buried in the ashes of the past. And yet, for Hitchcock at this moment, the old magnetic pull lived again. There wasn't another woman on the planet, only Ruby. All his progress in recovering from losing her was undone. He wanted her back.

"How come you were in a rat-hole like The Trunk Lid?" He asked. "Such places and people were beneath you only four years ago."

The softness in her eyes hardened. "Need I remind you, that four years ago, we had plans for marriage and family. If you remember, I loved you. Maybe I still do. But we've changed, Roger. Me more than you, and you know *why*."

Her words hit him like a slap in his face. He looked carefully at her. This wasn't the woman who had been his fiancée; the sweet, innocent transplant from Mississippi. Everything about her now announced her as an amoral woman, and a bitter radical also.

"Daddy says to tell you 'hello' for him, by the way," she said. "He never approved of you having darkies for friends, but he admired you for excelling against them in boxing. He was pleased when I told him you're a police officer now, like he was back in Mississippi."

Hitchcock grinned at the memory of the man he once thought would be father-in-law. "Say 'hello' to Burl for me too. I remember he told me he took a lot of heat for being the first man in his family who didn't join the Klan, so I guess he would be upset over the color of some of my friends."

"You and Daddy always got along so well. You were his pick for me."

"Tell him I still have the .38 he gave me and taught me to shoot. Tell him I carried it with me every day I was in 'Nam and it saved my life and others several times."

"I will," she said, smiling. "He'll be pleased to know that he helped."

They both paused. He felt the power of her sensuality melting him.

"Your 'Dear John' letter to me when I was over there almost got me killed," he said. "But this is now. What about us, Ruby? I still love you. I don't need to think about it. I do. You only. Don't you miss what we had? Was what happened so bad that we can't pick up the pieces and pick where up we left off?"

She shook her head and locked her eyes on his. "I'm sorry my letter put your life at risk. That was never my intention." She paused, never breaking his gaze. "The old me is dead. Think about it, Roger. We would have had twin boys. *Ours.* You were my first man, you would have been my only man, but you abandoned me, you went off to war when you didn't have to. If you married me you could have stayed home, when I needed you."

He looked down into his half-empty cup of coffee, now cold. He was unable to say anything. Inside he was bleeding. He knew Ruby had more to say. She was bitter, but he listened.

"I loved your dad," she went on. "He was a wonderful man, but to be by myself with two babies while you were away in the Army, being around your mom with her disapproval of me, would have been too much. I wanted a family with you. Lots of kids, to settle down, help you through medical school, even if we had to be poor for a while. But no, you had to go off killing communists."

Seeing and hearing Ruby's pain and anger brought Hitchcock to the point of fighting tears. He lowered his head, hands on the table. Grieved by his actions, he had no words.

"You changed overnight when your father died," Ruby continued. "The war was heating up, and you and your friends were hot-to-trot to get over there to fight. You left me defenseless against your mother's schemes after the abortion. You didn't marry me and take care of me. Your rejection changed me into what I am now. I never thought I would, but I *like* who I am now, Roger."

"And who are you now, Ruby?" he asked, fearing the answer.

She paused, as if she didn't want to answer, then said, "It's not just *who* I am, but also *what* I am. The opposite of you. I smoke pot, Roger. I think it should be legalized. I like cocaine, and I think it should be legalized. I go to peace demonstrations and I date different men, lots of them. To put it in old-fashioned terms you will understand, I am mistress to both owners of the Trunk Lid. For the moment, at least."

Hitchcock's heart jumped to his throat again. "What do you get out of the arrangement?" A question he had to ask.

She looked at him, surprised by the question. "My expenses, all the pot and cocaine I want, and a nice car of my own, lots of spending money. I might try LSD next, I'm not sure."

He sat back in his seat, astonished. As if she couldn't cause more dismay, she did. He realized she was taunting him with her current situation with two men. That hurt him bad enough, but her talk of dabbling with LSD warranted a response. Shaking his head solemnly, he warned her "Whatever you do, Ruby, don't go near acid, not even once."

Ignoring his warning, she said "I don't want marriage. I don't want kids. The traditional family is outdated anyway," she said, changing the subject. "The whole country's changing except you, and your kind. You think the Watts riots were something? You think the war protests are something? The next waves of protest will be bigger, by people of color–Mexicans, Indians, and Asians. Women too. It's not just blacks anymore who will demonstrate against the Establishment. The old order is dying."

Her words hit him like a Mack truck. The depth of her bitterness and turn her to dangerous drugs, promiscuity and protest politics shocked him. There could be no going back now. As a police officer, a lawman, being with Ruby, a druggie and a radical, would compromise his career. She had crossed the line. Hitchcock realized the love between them, faint as it felt a moment ago, couldn't be. Ever again.

"For what it's worth, Ruby, I didn't reject you. You knew that, abortion or not, I would have married you. Yes, I was wrong to have not married you then. If I could do it over, I would still have joined the Army to fulfill my duty. But I would have married you first, had our kids and by this time I would be out. We'd be parents, raising a family in our own home. The abortion was wrong. We both know it now. But no one forced you to go through with it. Even so, I will ask you now...will you forgive me?"

Hurt, bitter eyes answered him before words. "Yeah, why not. Won't change anything."

Hitchcock's eyes met hers. "So why did you want to see me?"

She shrugged. "When I saw you Saturday night, I felt something. I felt it again when I first got here. But what I am now is where I'm at."

He stood and reached into his jeans pocket. "How much is a cup here?"

"Just went up to two bits, I guess."

Leaving a buck on the table, he walked Ruby to her car. She turned to him. "I won't deny that I love you still, Roger. Maybe we could go for it again, pick up the pieces, after I'm over this streak I'm on."

His eyes narrowed. "What's this you're saying–you want me to wait for you until you get your fill of other men, like the lyrics to the song 'Save the Last Dance for Me?' No thanks. I've tried to get you back and struck out," he said. "After two times at bat, I'm out, and better off."

He got in his El Camino and drove away. He glanced in his rearview mirror to see Ruby wiping tears from her cheeks as she watched him go.

Despite the powerful mixture of emotions and memories that dominated his drive back to Bellevue, an emotional numbness swept over him. Ruby's offer was a shock. It proved they are different people now; they had taken incompatible, irreversible life paths. He felt a sense of release and satisfaction in knowing that he had done what he could to make things right and win her back, but the only door she opened was one no man would accept.

He asked himself if he would start over, pick up the pieces if she had said yes. The answer was probably not. She wasn't the same girl he fell in love with. The Ruby he knew would never be mistress to two men for money and drugs and brag about it.

He felt horrible, condemned for his betrayal of the woman he loved and his children in her womb. The love he shared with Ruby was gone. He'd tried to get her back and failed. He was done. He accepted the end now. *Some things aren't meant to be, and never will*, became his realization. At last he could get on with his life. Or could he? The abortion and the unanswerable "what if" would probably haunt him for the rest of his days.

He liked the idea of loving again and building a family, but he was past wanting that for himself. All he had now were passing desires for Ruby, which were triggered by any attractive woman who passed under his eyes. He and other women were merely ships passing in the night. It seemed somehow significant that the rain had stopped by the time he had returned to his digs. He let Jamie out, feeling as if he had been turned upside down and shaken until empty.

His solace and only steady passion now was police work, but would it be enough to keep him from driving through life, looking in the rearview mirror?

CHAPTER ELEVEN
A Strange Hush Before the Storm

CAPTAIN ERIK DELSTRA arrived at the station at his usual time. As he expected every morning following a weekend, the inbox on the outside of his office door was filled to capacity. He found even more reports and a sealed manila envelope marked URGENT: FOR YOUR EYES ONLY under his office door.

He dialed Lydia, his administrative assistant. "Hold all calls unless it's the Chief, or Dennis Holland."

For the next two hours Delstra read officers' reports on the events and arrests at The Trunk Lid. He chuckled when he read of Walker's breaking the hand of the bouncer who tried to punch him, and of Otis Hitchcock's surprise return there and catching two heroin users in the act of shooting up.

Reading the accounts of the officers' exploits made Delstra, a Korean War era Marine, feel left out, wishing he could turn back the clock and get in on the action the new generation of officers faced.

He made a note to contact the state Liquor Board and the City business licensing department to demand the suspension or revocation of The Trunk Lid's liquor and business licenses.

After reading Forbes' report, and the reports of the off-duty officers who saved him from the crowd, Delstra remembered the comments he had heard from other Patrol commanders regarding Forbes' aggressiveness toward arrestees. He decided to assess the risk to the Department if they keep Forbes on the force.

He read Sergeant Breen's memo, recommending Hitchcock for a service commendation for reviving a drug addict who was clinically dead and taking him to the hospital. Attached to the same report was a letter from the man's mother, Barbara Fowler, thanking the Department for Officer Hitchcock saving her son, who was dead when he arrived at her home.

Next, Delstra opened the sealed manila envelope, an interoffice memo with a handwritten note from Sergeant Breen on top:

> *Erik,*
> *I happened to find this memo lying open on Lt. Bostwick's desk. I took the liberty of copying it for you. I returned the original to Rowland. He does not know you have a copy.*
> *Jack*

Delstra's blood boiled when he read Bostwick's memo to one of the young assistant city managers Delstra referred to as "young Bolsheviks." Bostwick's memo described his meeting with Hitchcock, whom he accused of "gross insubordination" and: *Often exhibits strong indications of antisocial behavior, with homicidal tendencies stemming from his military service in Vietnam, where he was engaged in killing, probably helpless peasants and women. Part of his service file is sealed, indicating he has something to hide.*

Bostwick ended his narrative, stating that he felt the Department's policy of giving hiring preference to veterans like Hitchcock, whom he described as "dangerous and should be dismissed," and the hiring and retention of veterans is "a troubling mistake," which he will correct when he becomes the Department's next chief. Bostwick concluded, stating he would take steps to ensure Hitchcock's eventual termination.

Delstra had long been suspicious of Bostwick, a poor fit in the Department, who made a point of standing apart from everyone else, as if he wanted no one to know him. Bostwick's assignments to administration instead of Patrol or Traffic baffled everyone below chief or deputy chief. Bostwick had never made an arrest on his own, yet his perfect promotion test scores and rapid rise through the ranks astonished his peers. Until now his intentions and loyalties were never clear.

Having read the confidential memo, Delstra resolved to protect Hitchcock from the clutches of Bostwick, uncover the other conspirators and deal with each accordingly.

Another envelope from Sergeant Breen contained two more memos. The first was from Hitchcock, to Sergeant Breen, reporting that the mother of the heroin addict whose life he saved, had named Tyrone Guyon as the source of the heroin. Hitchcock's memo further stated that Guyon is well known to the Seattle Police as a heroin dealer and a convicted felon. Hitchcock named two people who died on the same night in Bellevue from heroin, believed to have been supplied by Guyon in the last week.

The other memo was from Breen to himself, stating the felony warrants for Guyon had been confirmed, adding that Guyon is known to be armed at all times, and to turn women into addicts to force them into prostitution for him. Breen had briefed the entire patrol, traffic and detective divisions and posted Guyon's mug shot in the squad room.

DELSTRA FLIPPED THROUGH the thin stack of citizen complaints about officers' use of force in making arrests at The Trunk Lid. None were about excessive force, but rather officers' attitudes. He would handle each one with a phone call after more pressing matters were handled.

He leaned back in his chair, reflecting on what he had read, thinking that what his officers currently faced were vastly different than what his generation encountered just six years ago. Big city crime had crept into the suburbs, taking advantage of an unaware, naïve, and often well-to-do populace. Drug dealers, prostitutes and pimps, armed robberies and attacks on officers were happening in the suburbs now. Bellevue was not immune, yet the city leaders seemed determined to keep their heads buried in the sand.

Delstra was also aware that his officers faced a danger that the Seattle cops didn't, the mind-numbing boredom of routine patrol in quiet suburbs and small towns where nothing happens. Around the country, officers who routinely face the same quietude day after day are dying or are seriously injured because of a deadly 'nothing ever happens here' mindset.

Officers in the suburbs don't get enough intense activity or training on a consistent basis to develop the dominance and the survival edge they need to prevail when the chips are down.

Delstra had read the FBI's statistics that over half of the officers killed in the line of duty last year were from suburban towns and rural counties. But no one on the city council or the city manager's office seemed to notice or care.

Bellevue wasn't experiencing a crime wave, but the

recent rise in crime overall had been sharp and more violent. Much of it could be attributed to recent, massive annexations which quadrupled and diversified the population and square miles of jurisdiction in a short time. Major changes were occurring not only on the streets, but within the Department.

As the Department grew to meet the new demands being placed on it, so did the turmoil within. Political factions sprang up, conspiring against each other and the gossip and rumors became ugly. The Department's small town, family environment was no more.

The attitudes of most of the Brass frustrated Delstra. Their unwillingness to acknowledge that the increase in crime occurring across the country has reached Bellevue as it has everywhere else. Officers were frustrated that lieutenants and captains tended to side with citizens who complained against officers.

It also troubled Delstra that the older generation, his own, didn't acknowledge the need to modernize training, equipment, and operations to meet the new challenges. No one in the Brass except himself, not even the Chief, protested the closure of the shooting range four years ago. The decision-makers upstairs, and the majority of the elected council members ignored his repeated warnings of the enormous liability the City faces by having officers carry guns without standardized, regular training and qualifications.

Delstra wondered, *what will it take for the city council*

to wake up and take action?

As he sat back in his chair and reflected on the matter, he sensed a change of some sort was around the corner.

CHAPTER TWELVE
The Work of the New Mata Hari

THE MESSAGE IN Hitchcock's inbox when he came to work was marked urgent. It read: CALL MATA AT 9:00 P.M. SHARP.

He had code-named Gayle after Mata Hari, the woman spy of WWI fame, a beautiful exotic dancer who blew a kiss to her firing squad moments before she was executed by the French army for being a double agent.

Not only did Gayle resemble Mata Hari in the physical sense, she was as daring and alluring as the spy had been. Gayle wasn't an exotic dancer, but she was exotic. Her past was just as dark and steamy as the original Mata Hari. That, plus her firsthand knowledge of the underworld qualified her well for spy-work.

With no calls holding, he rolled out of the station in his black-and-white, headed for the Fowler residence.

The usual squalor and unpleasant odors in the Fowler home were gone. The little starter home looked and smelled clean and neat. Barbara Fowler's countenance was the most peaceful he had ever seen, due, he figured, in large part to her oldest son's recent rescue from the Grim Reaper.

She greeted him with a warm smile.

"Hi, Mrs. Fowler. I stopped by to see how Randy is doing."

"So good of you to visit us, Roger," she said. "It means a lot. Randy's doing fine. He's in his room. Jim, my youngest, says 'thank you' and hopes to see you some time."

"I'd like to see Jim. Is he home?"

"He's at church. Youth group, but he'll be back later tonight."

"I'd like to say hello to Randy, if he's up. May I come in?"

"He's up and he'd be thrilled that you came. You know the way, son."

He headed down the hall and knocked at Randy's door. Randy was sitting up in bed, rail-thin and sickly, but Hitchcock was grateful to see him alive and improving.

"Roger!" he exclaimed, leaning forward. "Didn't expect to see you so soon. You saved my life, man! I'll never be able to repay you."

Hitchcock settled on the chair next to the bed. "Glad you made it, Randy. You had a very close call. I hope you never go back to that stuff now that you're clean. I hate losing friends."

"I'm on a good program, by court order," Randy said. "Mom worked a deal with the prosecutor to get me outpatient treatment. There'll be meetings with a counselor, and all that. If I complete the program and stay clean for a year, the charge stays off my record."

Hitchcock nodded. "I'm glad to hear it, Randy."

"I'll be going to church with Mom and Jim, and I still might get that job at Lake Hills Chevron. If I do, I can walk to work. Without a car to keep up, I can save money. All this is possible thanks to you, buddy."

The peace on Randy's face and in his eyes told Hitchcock his friend was sincere.

He checked his watch. "Sorry to cut this short, Randy, but I have an appointment in fifteen minutes. Gotta go."

Randy extended his hand. "Got some far-out cop stuff to do, huh? Be careful, Roger."

Shaking hands, he replied, "I'll come back in a couple days, Randy. Take care."

A familiar tingle of anticipation went through Hitchcock as he drove away from Randy's house.

AT EXACTLY 9:00 p.m. he called the number he was given from a pay phone in front of the Lake Hills QFC store. Gayle answered on the first ring.

"Roger?"

"Hi, Gayle. It's me. Whatcha a got?"

She sounded excited when she said, "The latest on Tyrone Guyon! My source at the Hilltop told me today that Guyon is in and out of there all the time now, hangs out at the bar. He's got a white girl with him most of the time. A blonde, name's Mae. She drives him around, dominates the other girls Tyrone brings to the motel. She beats them to make sure they do as he says. She does everything for him."

"What kind of wheels should I be looking for?"

"Two. Mostly he drives an older white Lincoln, a big boat with fancy wheels. But as of today, Guyon is driving a green Ford Maverick."

Hitchcock felt his pulse spike. "Where was the Maverick seen last?"

"At the Hilltop about three hours ago."

"Anything else?"

"Yes—watch yourself, Roger. Guyon showed a revolver to one of the cleaning maids yesterday, a young colored girl, as his way of impressing her. He's been giving her small amounts of pot and cocaine. She's pretty, so he wants her to work for him. To impress her, he told her he's going to kill a white cop with his gun."

"So where is Guyon now? Does your friend know that?"

"Nope, 'cept he's got two places. One in the Seattle Central District, the other is a house somewhere in Eastgate, close by, on the south side of the freeway. My source said that because the Seattle cops are looking for him, Guyon is almost always in Eastgate now."

"A house!" he echoed excitedly. "I didn't know any of this. Anything else? Like when does he go to the Hilltop? Where else does he go in Bellevue? Is today the first time she saw him in the green Maverick?"

"Don't have any of that at the moment, Roger. Only that he's in Bellevue now more than Seattle. Sorry. I'm working to get more. I'll call you the second I have anything else."

"Time is of the essence, Gayle. This guy is killing people by deliberate overdose. You already have my number. I'm giving you our emergency number in case you learn where he is. Tell them to call me so I can call you. How late are you working tonight?"

"I'm here until closing at two. I'm going straight home then."

Hitchcock wasted no time writing up Gayle's information on a standard report form and taking it to Sergeant Breen at the station. Breen read it carefully while he waited.

"How did you get this?" Breen asked.

"My informant. I told you about her."

Breen shook his head in dismay, "I can't believe this is happening in Bellevue, but it is. I've got to alert the rest of the squad right away. I'll meet each one in person so the reporters who monitor our frequencies won't know. Find this guy, Roger. And for God's sake, keep me posted and be careful."

"I have no doubt her information is correct, Jack. I trust her."

Hitchcock returned to District Six, keeping on the move, checking and re-checking parking lots and bars for either the white Lincoln or the green Mustang. Nothing.

He heard Sergeant Breen radio each of the other officers, one after another, for a meeting. *Jack's making sure everyone has information about Guyon, the descriptions of his vehicles, his armed status and his stated intentions to kill a white officer in case anyone happens to see Guyon in either of his vehicles. If they do, they'll know to call for backup.*

Feeling edgy, he stopped by the Wagon Wheel to see for himself that Gayle was there. "Nothing new yet," she muttered under her breath as she passed him on her way to a table with a tray of drinks.

He checked the parking lot of the Hilltop. Neither the white Lincoln nor the green Maverick were there. He ran the plate of every car or truck there for warrants. No hits. The lounge had few customers.

Like the Hilltop, the Steakout parking lot was almost empty. Two men walked out the second Hitchcock entered to say hello to the bartender. The employees outnumbered the customers, the cleanup crew came in and started unpacking their equipment. Seeing the place would close early, he chatted with the bartender as he washed glasses, wiped down the bar and closed out the till.

When Hitchcock returned to his cruiser, he discovered the driver door window of his cruiser was smashed out. He assumed it was an act of malice by the two who left when he entered the bar.

He notified Sergeant Breen of the damage. "Leave it at the city garage, take the shotgun with you. I'll have Sherman pick you up. You'll ride with him the rest of the shift," Breen replied.

Sherman arrived at the garage minutes after Hitchcock. "Looks like we're a two-man unit for the rest of the shift, Roger," Sherman said, grinning as usual.

"Yeah, it's been so quiet it gives me the creeps. Like something big is gonna happen," Hitchcock said as he placed the shotgun from his car and his briefcase in the trunk of Sherman's cruiser.

"Yeah? Is this your gut instinct I keep hearing about?" Sherman asked, only half- joking.

"Probably... Maybe," he replied, shaking his head. "It just feels like something's gonna happen."

Sherman laughed. He was one of the handsomest men on the Department. Tall and lean like Hitchcock, but on a lighter frame and built like a gymnast and an aristocratic stamp about him. Though happily married, Sherman's looks, approachable demeanor and full head of prematurely silver hair drew women to him like flies to honey.

"Uh-oh!" said Sherman, still half-joking. "The word is out that something always happens when you get *that* feeling. I better recheck my weapon. Maybe we'll get into a gun battle tonight. Wouldn't miss that for anything!"

"Okay, Tom," Hitchcock said, brushing Sherman's jokes aside. "Call us in and let's go to Eastgate. We're on the lookout for Tyrone Guyon."

Sherman nodded cheerfully, as if he had been invited to a ball game. "Yeah. Breen briefed me about him," he said.

"So, are we Three Zero Five, or Six?"

"Why not call in as Three Fifty-Six and see what Radio says?"

"I kind of like Three Sixty-Five better," Hitchcock quipped.

"We better call in as something before Breen gets upset," Sherman said, chuckling.

Joking aside, Hitchcock knew that Sherman was another officer who believed in the accuracy of his gut instincts. He rechecked his revolver and spare ammunition pouches before leaving the city garage, then keyed his radio mic: "Three Zero Five to Radio, 10-8 with Three Zero Six on board as a two-man unit covering Districts Five and Six."

"*Received. Three Zero Five is now a two-man unit, back in service at 2340 hours,*" the dispatcher acknowledged.

Sherman driving, they returned to Eastgate to hunt for Tyrone Guyon.

† † †

A FEW MINUTES past midnight, Tyrone Guyon awoke in the ramshackle little rental house in Eastgate, alone except for the new girl he had locked up in a spare bedroom after shooting her up with the third dose of heroin a few hours ago.

He had been snorting cocaine for two days until he finally crashed. He could count on Mae to keep the other girl, Linda, busy in his trailer in the trailer park next to the Hilltop while he slept.

Guyon felt the dreaded cravings coming. He made a desperate search through his and Mae's clothes and the bathroom. He was out. He counted his cash before he called Marcellus. He had only a thousand, not enough. He knew that when Mae brought the money Linda earned tonight in the trailer, there should be enough to buy for his own needs, plus more to sell. Provided, that is, that Linda didn't try to hold back some of the money for herself, like she tried to do two days ago.

He called Marcellus's number and hung up on the third ring. That was the code to signal Marcellus who was calling. When he called back, Marcellus picked up but only listened until Guyon identified himself.

"Be at the same place as last time. One o'clock, with the cash," Marcellus told him. The call ended.

Moments later Tyrone's phone rang. He stared at it, waiting. After the second ring, it stopped. Then it rang again. That was Mae's signal.

"How much?" he asked when he picked up the phone.

"Sixteen hundred, total," Mae reported. "Linda wanted her share, but I told her what she gets, if anything, after last time, is up to you."

"Okay. Get here quick. We're goin' to meet Marcellus. Bring Linda with you for extra insurance. We'll make him think he can buy her from us."

"We're going to sell her?" Mae asked.

"Hurry. That Marcellus, he gets suspicious when anybody's late."

After two days of snorting cocaine without sleep, paranoia dominated Tyrone's thought processes, even after dozing for several hours. A believer in the spirit realm, he became convinced that spirits were warning him that someone was out to kill him. He didn't know who. Someone or something other than the police. The Seattle cops would kill him on sight.

Suddenly, in his drug-addled brain, the spirit realm told him Marcellus had turned snitch. Tonight, he'd get Marcellus's guard down, shoot him, take his dope and his money and leave his body for the cops to find.

He thought about the risks of going into Seattle as he checked his revolver, making sure it was loaded with "cop-killer" rounds, hollow-point bullets.

The Seattle bulls would be watching for his white Lincoln, so taking it there would be too risky. He decided to go in the dead girl's car, the green Maverick.

Thanks to Mae, it had newly stolen plates on it.

He loaded both barrels of his sawed-off shotgun and put two extra shells in his jacket pocket. He tucked his revolver in his front waistband. Any cops he saw tonight would be dead meat.

He checked the girl in the back bedroom. She was still sleeping. He nodded with satisfaction as he eased the door closed and snapped the padlock shut. *Can't risk her escaping; not after all we went through to bring her here. When she wakes up, she'll be ready to make me a lot of money.*

Mae arrived in the Lincoln with Linda, a slender, meek girl in her early twenties with mouse-brown hair, in the front passenger seat.

Tyrone backed the Maverick out of the single-car garage, then parked the Lincoln inside and closed the door. He handed Mae the key to the Maverick, and told her, "Marcellus' place. You drive. Linda in front so he can see her. I'll lay low in the back, out of sight until we meet Marcellus. The Seattle pigs won't bother two white chicks and they don't know this car."

Mae checked her purse gun, a compact Colt .380 caliber automatic, making sure its magazine was full with hollow-point bullets. Guyon opened the right rear door and laid on the floor, his head behind the driver seat, cradling the sawed-off 12-gauge shotgun on his lap, the.38 in his waistband.

"One more thing," Guyon said to Mae, "We kill any cop who stops us tonight. I'll be in the back. You just pull over and tell me where they comin' from. We'll shoot Marcellus tonight, too."

Mae patted her handbag. "I'm ready."

Tyrone leaned in and whispered in Mae' ear "You keep an eye on Linda."

She checked her short, bleached hair in the mirror as she got in the driver seat. She gave a hard stare at Linda. "You're our bait tonight. Buckle your seat belt and don't say anything unless me or Tyrone speaks to you," she said harshly.

"I'm in need," Linda pleaded, her voice breaking.

Mae reached into her purse, took out her pocket-sized pistol and pressed the barrel against Linda's head. "You get more when we say. We're gonna see how much we can get for you. Now buckle up so we know you won't escape."

Linda's hands trembled as she snapped the seat belt over her lap. Mae glared at her as she cinched Linda's belt tight, then drove through the sleeping neighborhood to the freeway overpass.

HITCHCOCK AND SHERMAN sat in the Steak Out parking lot in view of the freeway overpass, sharing Army experiences to ease the tension they both felt. They were talkative in the way of men who wait for a battle to begin.

"You were in the Rangers, a paratrooper, weren't you?" Hitchcock said. "Never could stand heights myself. Above seven or eight feet on a ladder gives me butterflies, so I became a medic."

Sherman nodded, keeping his eyes on the streets. The paratrooper in him wouldn't let him get too relaxed. Plus, Sergeant Breen alerting him about Tyrone Guyon wanting to kill a white officer, and Hitchcock's gut instinct acting up convinced him something was coming down.

Like most veterans, Sherman didn't talk much about what he did while in the military. In itself, this seemed a strange trait. Rather than shame, as some might think, the reluctance to talk about their service was the mark of men who had nothing to prove to anyone. But this night, given the information they had, and where they were, talking about his Army days with Hitchcock, a fellow ex-soldier, calmed Sherman and kept him on alert at the same time.

"Heights never bothered me," Sherman said with his signature smile, "but the training to get into the 101st was the toughest thing I ever did. Eighty percent washout rate; our muscle mass was gone after the final days of what they call hell week. But the effect of being in an elite unit had on women made it worthwhile like you wouldn't–"

"Hey Tom!" Hitchcock interrupted, pointing ahead. "Is that a green Maverick crossing the overpass, heading toward us?"

"Yeah! Definitely a Maverick," Sherman replied.

"My informant told me tonight Guyon has a place in lower Eastgate, and we believe the girl who owned the Maverick got her heroin from Guyon. A black male was seen driving it from the victim's apartment about the time she died."

"Can't tell the color from here in this light," Sherman said. He dropped the gear shift into Drive. "I'll get close, you get the plate and run it. Hang on!"

Sherman sped out of the Steak Out parking lot to the north end of the overpass and flashed his high beams to see the front plates on the approaching Maverick as he passed it heading in the opposite direction.

"Got it?"

"Yep." Hitchcock switched to Channel Two. "Three Zero Five, Records, this is urgent. Run a registration check 10-28 on Ocean Zebra Paul, Six Two One, Washington plate."

Sherman hung a U-turn. "That's gotta be it. It's not only green, it even has the damaged left fender. And those two broads are very nervous."

"Stay with them, Tom."

"Oh yeah!"

MAE DRISCOLL PANICKED when she saw in her rearview mirror the Bellevue black-and-white make a U-turn. She missed the on-ramp to the westbound freeway and had to stop at the red traffic signal facing the T-intersection. Not knowing what to do next, her pulse raced as the patrol car came up behind her.

"Tyrone, we got trouble!" she shouted.

"Talk to me! What's goin' on? I can tell you didn't make that turn to the freeway," Guyon shouted from the rear floor.

Mae's heart was racing. "Bellevue PD right behind us! Two pigs in the car!"

"Damn! Get us outta here! Drive! Drive!" Guyon shrieked, panicking.

Mae froze. Terrified. She sat through a green signal, the police car remaining right behind her. As the signal turned to red again, she suddenly turned left against the red light into the intersection, heading toward the Steak Out. Panic consumed Mae Driscoll by the second.

RECORDS CAME BACK with the report: *"Three Zero Five, the license plate Ocean Zebra Paul Six Two One is stolen. Belongs on a white 1966 Chevy Malibu, registered owner in Seattle."*

Sherman activated the overhead red light.

"Three Zero Five received," Hitchcock acknowledged.

Hitchcock's heart pounded as he said, "That's it, the Maverick belonging to Janine Collins. I only see the two women, though, no man on board."

Sherman kept the same distance of two car lengths behind the Maverick as it turned left on 148th Avenue for a block, then right on the empty frontage road, at speeds below the posted limit.

Instead of pulling over, the Maverick continued westbound on the two-lane frontage road, weaving erratically, crossing the center line and back again in a herky-jerky fashion, increasing speed.

"Looks like the women are fighting! They missed the last on-ramp if they're trying to get to Seattle," Sherman exclaimed.

Hitchcock switched back to Channel One. "Three Zero Five Radio, request assistance stopping a suspected stolen vehicle. Green sixty-nine Ford Maverick, dented fender, bearing stolen Washington plates Ocean Zebra Paul Six Two One. Headed westbound on the Highway 10 north frontage road, passing Lakeside Sand and Gravel. Two white females aboard!"

Sergeant Breen came on the air: *"Four Twenty is en route to assist Three Zero Five, Radio."*

Then Dispatch came on the air: *"10-4. All units, emergency traffic only."*

The Maverick and Sherman's patrol car were the only vehicles on the frontage road when Sherman sounded the siren. At thirty miles per hour the Maverick swerved over the centerline again below a crest in the hill, then over-corrected to the right, and crashed head-on into a telephone pole.

Sherman aimed his spotlight at the Maverick's rear window, flooding the interior with light. The heads of two occupants in the front seat could be seen; neither moved.

"They gotta be hurt after a crash like that," Hitchcock said.

"Probably unconscious," Sherman said. "You're the former medic. Let's go check 'em."

Hitchcock keyed the radio mic: "Three Zero Five, radio, suspect vehicle just crashed into a telephone pole on the frontage road in front of Lakeside Sand and Gravel. The occupants in the front seat are visible but aren't moving. We'll be checking for injuries. Get Flintoff's on the way."

Hitchcock and Sherman stepped out of the cruiser. They stood, watching the heads of the two in the front seat, the driver a blonde, the passenger had light brown hair. Neither moved. Steam rose into the air from the radiator. The medic in Hitchcock wanted to check on the two women. Surely, they were hurt.

He and Sherman exchanged glances, then moved forward as one man, shining flashlights into the rear window. Their shadows from their spotlight preceded them they walked up to the wrecked vehicle from the rear. Hitchcock on the right, Sherman on the left. Hitchcock saw the driver's head turn as he and Sherman reached the rear bumper of the Maverick.

Suddenly the rear window exploded, splattering the chests of both officers with lead pellets and glass fragments. Hitchcock drew his gun and opened fire first at the black male adult on the rear floor aiming a double-barrel shotgun at them, about to fire again. Sherman began firing at a burst of light and a gunshot that came from the front seat as Hitchcock continued shooting at the man with the shotgun.

During the ferocious exchange of gunfire at pointblank range, both officers descended to the lowest level of their training. Vision narrowed to a tunnel as they returned fire without thought. Their heart rates rocketed as they watched the man with the shotgun in the back seat aiming at them, about to fire the other barrel.

The shotgun and the man on the other side of it were all there was in Hitchcock's tunnel of vision. Nothing existed but to kill the man before he could fire the shotgun again. He saw a flash from the driver seat, then a second loud explosion from the shotgun, and suddenly Hitchcock was clicking an empty trigger. In his peripheral vision he saw Sherman clicking his trigger. Empty guns. *Danger remains. Go for cover—reload!*

He stepped backward three steps, opened the cylinder of his service revolver. Six empty shells tinkled as he shucked them onto the pavement, walking backward in a half-crouch, staying abreast of Sherman, eyes on the Ford Maverick.

As he reached the protection of the cruiser, Hitchcock's mind flashed back to the ambush of four California Highway Patrol officers who died in an ambush in the Newhall incident six months ago. One trooper had taken cover behind his cruiser and was shot in the head while reloading his revolver.

Hitchcock opened the passenger door and knelt behind it to reload. He mentally cursed the city for the inadequate equipment it provided as he opened one ammo pouch on his gun belt and only three rounds came out. His fingers were stiff from fear, adrenalin and the cold. He managed to extract three more rounds from his other ammo pouch to finish reloading.

He glanced at Sherman, kneeling behind the driver door, his gun already reloaded.

"You okay, Roger?" Sherman asked, keeping his eyes on the Ford Maverick.

Hitchcock remained kneeling behind the door, gun aimed at the Maverick. He took a couple seconds to check himself over with his left hand. "I'm not hurt, Tom! I see movement in the front passenger seat!"

"I'm okay, too," Sherman said as he grabbed the radio mic. "Shots fired, Radio! Officers not hurt. One suspect believed dead!"

As reasoning and logic returned, Hitchcock became certain that the man in the back was dead and that he was Tyrone Guyon.

Sergeant Breen came on the air: "Four-Twenty is at the scene, Radio. Confirming shots fired, officers not hurt, one suspect believed dead. Get the on-call detective supervisor to send two detectives, get an ETA from Flintoff's, request a second unit from them and get the coroner on the way!"

Hitchcock again saw movement in the Maverick. He heard a woman wailing. "Help me! Oh God, somebody help me!"

From behind Sherman's cruiser, Sergeant Breen aimed his vehicle spotlight through the blown out rear window of the Maverick, illuminating the interior even more.

Hitchcock could see the heads of two occupants on the front seat. Breen came up behind Hitchcock. "Cover me as I approach the car," he said, urgency in his voice. "At least the passenger is alive."

Hitchcock and Sherman took positions on either side of the Maverick to cover Sergeant Breen as he approached on the right side. Hitchcock's eyes shifted between his sergeant and what he could see of the occupants of the Maverick, ready to fire if anyone inside tried to open fire again

Breen shone his flashlight into the interior, gun in hand. He had never seen anything like this in his eleven years on the job, nor during his two-year peacetime stint in the Army. "The man in the back is Tyrone Guyon, guys," Breen announced. "His face is shot up, but it's him."

Hitchcock stepped forward and peeked through the gaping hole in the back window. Sure enough, lying supine on the back floor; motionless, with a sawed-off double-barrel shotgun laying on his lap, was the man Hitchcock recognized from Seattle PD mugshots as Tyrone Guyon. Multiple gunshot wounds to his head distorted his face, his mouth hung open as if to express shock, his eyes were unseeing slits.

"Careful, Tom, she may only look dead," Hitchcock said as Sherman walked up the driver side and shone his flashlight on the blonde, motionless woman in the driver seat. From the other side of the car, Hitchcock shone his light on the driver. Deathly still, leaning forward, arms at her sides, head turned to the right, resting on the steering wheel, mouth open, eyes staring into eternity.

Sergeant Breen opened the passenger door. The moaning, writhing passenger looked at him as he reached over her to check the driver's right wrist for a pulse, and shook his head.

The slender young woman with brown hair in the front passenger seat slowly turned her head side to side, in agony, barely conscious. Eyes closed, lips open, her hands rested palms-up in her lap in a gesture of surrender. Blood saturated her lap. She mumbled something about getting another fix. Hitchcock stood next to Breen as he asked, "What's your name, miss?"

"Linda," she croaked, staring at Breen in a slack-jawed stupor, her eyes half-shut. "They've got another girl–in…their…house. Prisoner–until–hooked. *Got*–to–save–her," Linda pleaded with effort. She paused, then, "*Please*, don't tell Mae or Tyrone I told you... They'll kill me."

To Breen's surprise, a sense of bravado and gallows humor arose from within him. "Naw," he said matter-of-factly. "They won't be bothering anybody anymore, miss. I promise you that. They're both dead. Now, who is this girl and where is she?"

Linda's slowly lifted her head off the headrest and looked at Breen. "They're dead? Both dead? How? I can't believe it!"

"Believe it. They made the mistake of tangling with my boys. Now tell me who is the man in the back and where is the girl being held?"

Linda started to fade, her eyes half-closed. "Tyrone, Tyrone Guyon," she replied. "His house...small... brown...behind gas station... She's locked in a back room... Nice lady... You've *got* to check on her."

"We'll find her right away. What's her name?" Breen asked.

Linda's answers were slowing; her eyes were beginning to close. Her jaw hung open as she replied "Claudia...something. She's...missing from Everett," she slurred as she slipped into unconsciousness.

"I can go, Sarge," Hitchcock offered.

"Nope. You and Sherman were just involved in a shooting; you'll both stay until detectives get here."

Hitchcock looked at the passenger in the Maverick. "Let me help her. She's bleeding a lot through her clothes. Not a good sign."

"Go for it, Roger," Breen said.

The Flintoff men arrived. Breen told them to stand back. "This officer is a former Army medic," he told them. They stayed out of the way as Hitchcock leaned into the passenger side of the Maverick and carefully opened Linda's blood-drenched blouse.

"She's bleeding to death! Get me two first aid kits, quick!" Hitchcock commanded. Sherman ran to his cruiser, popped the trunk and ran back to Hitchcock. Sergeant Breen did the same. Applying a thick gauze compress from the first aid kit in Sherman's cruiser and another from Sergeant Breen's, Hitchcock shook his head grimly as he worked frantically to stop the bleeding. One compress after another became saturated and failed to stop the bleeding. At last the hemorrhaging slowed enough for him to tape a double compress over the two bullet holes in her side.

Hitchcock waved the Flintoff men in. "She'll need transfusions if she's going to make it. Get her to the ER as fast as you can!"

They loaded Linda onto a gurney, into the hearse and sped away, Officer LaPerle leading with lights and siren.

Sergeant Breen leaned into the driver door window of his cruiser and grabbed his radio mic. Staring at Hitchcock and Sherman next to him, he keyed his radio. "Four-Twenty to Three Zero Seven?"

Otis answered, "Three Zero Seven."

"Respond immediately to the scene here on the frontage road for an urgent detail. Code Two."

"Ten-four, Three Zero Seven, en route," Otis replied.

A NEWS REPORTER arrived, then another, then another. Breen was not amused that reporters were arriving before any detectives did. He warned the reporters to stay back as two more patrol cars arrived.

Breen looked into the blood-soaked front seat from the driver side with his flashlight. The back of the driver's clothing was drenched in blood. He saw a glint of metal on the front seat. They were two small shell casings. *These were fired tonight, but where's the gun?* he wondered.

TOM SHERMAN'S ADRENALIN rush began to subside as a familiar feeling of raw elation came over him. Once again, he felt intensely alive after surviving deadly combat. Instinctively his hand felt for his gun to re-snap the holster strap. His gun was there but the strap wouldn't close. He looked down. The leather strap was broken.

"See this, Roger?" Sherman said, grinning. "I drew my gun right through the leather strap. Next time we work together, and you get one of your gut feelings that something's gonna happen, I got dibs on the shotgun!"

A SELF-CONSCIOUS grin came across Hitchcock's face. He, too, had that familiar "Thank God it wasn't me" feeling of relief and gratitude to come out of the ordeal alive and unharmed. It wasn't new to him either that his senses were sharpest after a brush with death. Then he felt little granules on the chest pocket seams of his uniform shirt.

"Hey Tom," Hitchcock said, holding a few lead granules in his palm. "Lucky for us Guyon was using birdshot. We'd be hurt, or killed for sure if he had double-ought buck in his shotgun."

Sherman chuckled and nodded as if he had been told his shoelace was loose. That was Tom Sherman.

Hitchcock checked his holster; he too had drawn his gun right through the leather strap.

A FLASHING RED light in the distance caught Hitchcock's eye. It was Joel Otis, on the frontage road, approaching the scene, Code Two.

ACKNOWLEDGEMENTS

Special thanks to Larry Siferd, who first suggested the concept of writing actual police experiences as a series. And to my friend Will Marriott, an expert in the medical field, for contributing technical information regarding drug abuse and addiction. I am also grateful to various retired members of the Bellevue and Seattle Police Departments who helped me place major events in contained in this book in chronological order.

ABOUT THE AUTHOR

JOHN HANSEN draws from personal experience for most of his writing. Between 1966-1970 he was a Gunners Mate aboard a WWII vintage amphibious assault ship, running solo missions in and out of rivers and coastal waterways of South Vietnam and other places. As a patrol officer with the Bellevue Police Department, his fellow officers nicknamed him "Mad Dog" for his tenacity. After ten years on Patrol, he served eleven years in the Detective Division, investigating homicide, suicide, robbery, assault and rape cases. As a private investigator since retirement, his cases have taken him to other countries and continents. He is the winner of several awards for his books, short stories and essays.

Made in the USA
Middletown, DE
17 February 2021